Ever Beleño is a collector of old Hollywood memorabilia. He's also a fan of dead people. Mummies are his special passion, just like flying saucers are his roommate Johnny's particular obsession. Ever's dark and gothic world might be lonely, but after a heartbreaking split with his ex, he wants it no other way . . .until he visits the sold-out Mummies of the World exhibit.

As Ever studies one particular ancient Egyptian mummy, he experiences the odd, chilly sensation of somebody touching and following him. Every time he turns to look, he thinks it's handsome but obnoxious security guard Chris Coelho, who snuck Ever into the exhibit as a favor. Chris clearly wants the favor returned, but would the man really feel up Ever in public? Ever isn't sure, but then once he goes home, weird things continue happening.

Chris shows up everywhere, but he's suddenly sweet, silly, profound and . . . forgetful. After a torrid night of passion, Ever becomes hooked on the guy even as his feelings for Chris veer between desire and exasperation.

And then, the mummy Ever had been studying disappears from the exhibit. Could the events be connected? Could the spirit of the mummy have somehow followed him home? Is Ever losing his mind? Or is Chris really, as he says in a drunken moment, The Love God of Indian Frybread?

This book was previously published.

The Love God of Indian Frybread
Copyright © 2018 A.J. Llewellyn
ISBN: 978-1-4874-2242-4
Cover art by Martine Jardin

Published by eXtasy Books Inc or
Devine Destinies, an imprint of eXtasy Books Inc

Look for us online at:
www.eXtasybooks.com or www.devinedestinies.com

THE LOVE GOD OF INDIAN FRYBREAD

BY

A.J. LLEWELLYN

DEDICATION

To Rosie Grindstaff who suggested this idea for a book. May the mummies never follow you home. Love, A.J.

xoxo

CHAPTER ONE

Ever Beleño lay on his back, the stench of his surroundings clogging his nose as he stared up at his roommate. He raised his head with difficulty, feeling dazed and disoriented. He tried wiggling his toes and fingers. So far, so good. Nothing seemed broken . . . yet.

"You okay down there?" Jhonny hoisted himself up on the rim of the Dumpster, peering down at him.

"Okay? Are you crazy? I just fell in a pile of trash, for chrissakes!"

"Yeah, listen . . . we gotta hurry." Jhonny loomed up higher on the rim of the stinky container. Ever could hear his feet scrabbling for a hold on the slick exterior.

"Do you see the spaceship anyplace?"

Jhonny had a one-track mind. For a guy who lived daily with his mother's mistake (misspelling his name on his birth certificate), he could be amazingly focused when it came to idiotic things. With important life issues, not so much.

"Lemme check for broken bones." Ever sat up, gingerly peeling a putrid chicken leg off his arm. Eeew! "Wow. You know what? I think I'm okay."

"Yeah, yeah, good. Oh-oh . . ."

Ever glanced up at his roommate. "What do you mean, oh-oh?"

"Not to panic you or anything, dude, but there's a security guard coming. And it's the asshole."

Jhonny's face disappeared. Ever heard him drop to the ground, running as a second voice shouted, "Hey!"

Ever kept still, holding his breath. It wasn't difficult. Breathing in garbage fumes wasn't his idea of fun. He heard the security guard following his roommate and took the opportunity, as the footsteps receded, to look around. It shocked him when he found the spaceship under a pile of discarded boxes. They'd received an email that morning that Warner Brothers' prop shop was relocating and had tossed out props from the old TV show Lost in Space. Ever had initially resisted helping Jhonny sneak onto the studio's ranch property, namely because they'd been warned that their nemesis, Chris Coelho, was working security.

Technically speaking, they weren't breaking into the studio backlot since Jhonny had an access pass. Still, lolling around a garbage bin wasn't Ever's idea of a good time. He waited a few more minutes.

The long silence told him he was alone. He scooched forward, his fingers closing around the rim of the spaceship. He was ecstatic on one hand, disappointed on the other. The spaceship had looked amazing and, of course, huge, in the show's opening credits but looked tinny, small and very tacky here in the Dumpster. He flicked off bits of chicken from it and examined the spaceship, which really wasn't that small now that he had fully excavated it. It was about four feet in diameter. Painted silver, it had been made with love by somebody's hand forty years ago. He felt a stab of nostalgia seeing Jupiter II painted on the side. That was the name of the spaceship in the series. Holy cow. This was it. They'd really found it! After forty-eight years, the ship would be restored and lovingly displayed.

It was probably worth a fortune, but like all the other memorabilia in Hollywood, it was deemed disposable.

Hollywood had a short memory when it came to its history. Movie buffs like Ever and Jhonny kept the legends alive. He struggled with the spaceship. How the hell was he gonna get the four-foot monster out of the Dumpster on his own?

"Ever!"

He heard Jhonny's voice to his left.

"I fucking found it!" Ever whispered back.

"Fucking A!" Jhonny hoisted himself over the top of the blue beast again, his eyes wide and shiny when he saw the spaceship.

"Awesome!"

"Here, I'll pass it to you."

Ever held up the surprisingly heavy prop, noticing the small windows around the top half and the electrical cords dangling from its base. This was a real find. They could fix the lights and display it in their apartment.

"Shit. He's coming back." Jhonny grappled with the huge craft, then took off running, footsteps following him, hard.

"I see you!" Coelho shrieked.

Ever ducked back down inside the Dumpster. How the hell was he gonna get out? Jhonny had his hands full—literally—with the spaceship, and they'd done enough recon missions to have a long-standing plan in place. He was on his own getting out of here. He'd meet Jhonny back at the car, parked around the corner. No matter what, Jhonny wouldn't drive off without Ever. Getting the spaceship to the car now that they'd found it was the priority. It always was.

He waited a moment, making sure he no longer heard footsteps. Ever hoisted himself up over the rim of the Dumpster, his slippery, chicken-greased fingers sliding on the metal lip. He heard the sounds of running feet. It was now or never. He vaulted over the edge and took off running, down an alleyway and detouring straight into the front yard of Samantha Stevens's house from the old TV show Bewitched.

How apt. It was not only one of his favorite shows from the sixties, but sometimes he thought Jhonny was a little too . . . well . . . .er, bewitched, by those old classics. Their home was like a museum, for chrissakes. A big, gaudy altar to the god of dead TV families.

Ever threw himself behind a big, flowering hydrangea bush outside Samantha's house and watched the security guard turn a corner away from him, walkie-talkie in hand.

"I fucking lost him!" Coelho muttered as he passed by.

Ever cringed. Of all the security guards that patrolled the lot, why did it have to be Chris Coelho? He hated Jhonny and Ever with a vengeance. Chris Coelho had failed the police academy twice and was poised for a third shot at the entrance exam thanks to new state rules requiring more ethnic policing. He fit the criteria with his Mexican mom and Native American father. Of all the studio security guards, he was the best looking, but also the most obnoxious.

There had been a time when Ever had found Coelho attractive. He still did. Until the guy opened his mouth to speak.

His associates were the ones who tipped off Ever and Jhonny to memorabilia dumping. They mourned the wholesale disposal of old treasures. Coelho, however, seemed to care little for history. He also seemed to be on a mission to catch Ever, in particular, in the act of Dumpster diving. Ever settled down on the hard-packed, dry earth, surveying the street through the hydrangea's branches.

On Bewitched, this studio backlot posed as Morning Glory Circle. The house number, 1164. Across the road was the Kravitz house, from which snoopy Mrs. Kravitz watched Samantha run witchily amuck every week.

Mrs. Kravitz's house became *The Partridge Family* house in the 1970s, now painted yellow for some other show. Ever spotted the house from *I Dream of Jeannie,* and down the end was *Gidget's* house, but with a more modern façade.

This street, just off West Oak in Burbank, was Ever and

Jhonny's equivalent of Disneyland. As a kid, when his dad was still alive and brought him to work when he was assistant director on various shows in the late eighties, Ever always gravitated to what he still thought of as Morning Glory Circle.

Ever's dad had always had great stories about the old stars. He'd cried when actress Elizabeth Montgomery, with whom he'd maintained a long friendship, died of cancer. Everyone who worked on *Bewitched* had fond memories of the actors. His father had adored TV's Samantha and taught Ever to love and respect old Hollywood. And he did.

He and Jhonny had published three Hollywood memorabilia books complete with the real addresses of celebrities (unlike most of the phony Star Maps), making sure the old movie stars were dead or long since moved before printing the addresses. They also had photos of suicide and murder sites, some of their souvenir studio items, and other quirky tidbits. They were careful not to reveal too much about the souvenirs. Although technically speaking, stealing rubbish wasn't a crime, since the items were coveted by movie fans they waited for months before revealing they'd scored a new item, and they kept their home address very secret.

Here's Hollywood was due for its fourth edition soon. It made Ever feel good to know that people treasured the old stories and the old stars. He'd met many of them, interviewing them for the books. He stood now, brushing off his jeans, taking a look up and down Morning Glory Circle before slipping around the side of the house and into Samantha's backyard.

These houses were real, albeit, empty. The exteriors were well-maintained, just like real houses. They were all in damned fine shape. You could peer inside the windows past the window treatments and see lights and discarded gaffer tape on the bare floors. He walked around the backyard, remembering treasured moments such as the dodo bird and Endora running around turning people into toads . . . life seemed so simple and sweet on those TV shows. For a moment, he stood still, trying to inhale that feel-good vibe.

Ever could have sworn he felt it. And then he opened his eyes. Chris Coelho stood there, watching him, a sardonic look on his face.

"Oh, boy," Chris said, a smirk lifting his lips in a reptilian way. "Is this my frickin' lucky day, or what?"

Jhonny paced outside his sixteen-year-old Honda Accord. It had been the bane of his existence since the day he'd bought it two years ago. He'd had no idea when he'd been talked into the purchase by the aggressive Englishman who owned it that it was the most prized vehicle for car thieves. It had been stolen eight times already and each time came back in slightly worse condition.

The last time somebody took it, the thieves etched a large cross on the dashboard. People often asked him now if he was a Jesus freak.

No. He was just the unlucky owner of a 1994 Honda Accord, which topped the theft list each year in Los Angeles. He hoped one day the thieves would strip it bare so he could buy a new car. Anything but a damned Honda.

"At least it's here," he grumbled to himself. He never knew whether it would, or wouldn't be. One time it was inconveniently stolen while he was hiking up in Griffith Park, leaving him stranded after dark on a remote mountaintop.

He checked on the spaceship, snug in the backseat and glanced back toward Oak Street. His relief at seeing Ever coming around the corner became tempered with concern that his best friend in the whole world was limping.

"What the hell happened?" he asked.

"Coelho asked me on a fucking date. I ran. He tackled me."

"Jesus." Jhonny ran a hand through his hair. "How'd you get away from him?"

"I promised him a date tomorrow."

Jhonny gaped at him, shaking his head. "Oh, man. I can't let you do it. No spaceship is worth getting lumbered with that jerk."

Ever held up his hands. "It's okay. We're going to the museum to see the mummy exhibit." He looked ridiculously pleased.

Jhonny tried not to show his relief. Ever had been whining about seeing the Mummies of the World, but the whole idea creeped Jhonny out. None of their other friends had warmed to the idea either. Ever was the most handsome guy Jhonny knew. His dark hair and brilliant blue eyes were an unusual combination. Black Irish some people called it, but at the age of thirty, Ever was still nursing a broken heart. California could do that to a guy. Breakups in Tinseltown often involved money and, for Ever, the cost had been huge.

He felt a twinge of guilt watching Ever peel back a shirt-sleeve to examine his grazed elbow. Ever did so much for him, but the truth was, it had been excruciating going to the bodies exhibit with him a few years ago, especially when he discovered that the bodies used had been executed Chinese prisoners. Now Ever wanted to see mummified remains from all over the world.

"That sounds like a hot date," he quipped, unlocking the passenger door for Ever.

"Mummies are just people." Ever climbed into the passenger seat. He winced as he lifted his injured leg onto the floor.

"Think you sprained it?" Jhonny asked. When Ever nodded, Jhonny raced around to the driver's side. He fired up the Honda. They'd drop by his mom's restaurant for lunch. Ever loved his mom's pizza and she could ice his foot for him.

Ever sighed. "I can handle seeing the exhibit with him, but I'd much rather see it with you."

Jhonny ignored his friend's hopeful glance.

"I'd be too afraid of something following us home," Jhonny said. "Some ancient spirit."

"That's so crazy," Ever scoffed. "Hey, why are we going up Victory?"

"I thought we'd swing by Crazy Pie."

"Cool." The pained expression fled Ever's face.

"You just love dead people," Jhonny said.

Ever laughed. "Yeah, and you just love your aliens." He twisted himself around to look at the spaceship bouncing along in the backseat.

"It's in great shape." He turned back around again.

"I know, isn't it?" Jhonny paused. "Maybe we should drop it home first. You know this damned car is a magnet for thieves."

"Fine by me. I'll wait down here. You mind bringing me a bag of frozen peas?"

"No problem." Jhonny detoured down to Moorpark Street, clicking the garage door open to their triplex on Ledge Avenue. It had been a real find, this building, even if their landlady, Mrs. Zapel, was a horny, middle-aged bat who took Ever and Jhonny's continual rejection of her as a sign of encouragement.

He parked by the back stairs and raced up to the second-floor unit he and Ever shared, dropping the spaceship onto the carpeted floor. Man, it was huge. It took up more space than he'd first imagined. He stared it at for a moment. Oh well, he couldn't do anything about it now. He'd deal with it later. It smelled oddly of rancid chicken fat. He washed his hands in the kitchen sink then ran back downstairs and fired up the engine again.

"Forget something?" Ever asked him.

"No." *Thunk.* "Oh, shit. *Frozen peas.* Sorry, man. We'll be at the restaurant in a minute."

Ever said nothing, but the pained expression had returned. Jhonny headed back to Magnolia Boulevard, looking for street parking. He no longer parked in the restaurant lot because car thieves seemed to expect him as if Jhonny's car was their mobile secondhand parts dealership.

In the past month alone, he'd had his hubcaps, radiator, fan belt, and his CD player stolen in separate incidents. And this with a club, LoJack, and an alarm. Scratch that—the club had been stolen a couple of months before.

Jhonny sniffed. "Why do I smell greasy chicken?"

"It's all over me . . . and it was on the spaceship."

"Oh . . . I wondered. It made my hands greasy."

Ever grinned. "It made my whole body greasy. You may want to shampoo the backseat."

"Naw. Maybe the thieves'll get hungry and steal it."

Ever laughed as they cruised to a stop. He got out. His limp wasn't too bad, but Jhonny still felt guilty. Inside the pizza bar, his mom came to greet them.

"What did you do to him?" she asked Jhonny, an accusatory look on her face.

"Not his fault, Mrs. Gallo," Ever said. "I tripped and fell."

Her eyes narrowed. "How come you smell like . . ." She leaned into him. "Bad chicken?"

"Long story, Mrs. G."

"You had lunch someplace else?" The murderous cast to her eyes and hands-on-hips-stance would unnerve any guy, but a cleaver-carrying Italian mama petrified even her nearest and dearest.

Ever limped off to the bathroom, shouting, "Never! I'd

never cheat on you!" over his shoulder.

Jhonny ordered the Family Special, a large square pepperoni pizza and a couple of Cokes.

His mom brought an ice pack to the staff table where Jhonny now waited for Ever. The table was actually a booth with Naugahyde red benches. Crazy Pie, an ode to everything to do with pizza, was one of the oldest restaurants in LA and it was Jhonny Gallo's constant worry that his mom hadn't forgiven him for not wanting to follow in the family footsteps.

"Where did you eat?" she asked.

"We didn't eat."

"You don't like my cooking."

Oh, man . . . here we go.

"We adore your cooking," Ever said, joining them at the table, smelling of almond hand soap.

She smiled. Finally. "Good thing for you that you brought your appetite and that I keep ice packs handy."

"Thanks, Mrs. G." Ever took it, a look of bliss crossing his face as he put his injured foot across the bench and the ice pack right on it.

"I keep telling you to call me Rosa."

Ever nodded. She did and he never would. He was a respectful guy.

Had Jhonny put his feet on her bench there'd be hell to pay. On the other hand, having Ever with him meant that his mom would drop the subject of his future in pizza-slinging, which she was wont to do when Jhonny was alone. Plus, she loved Ever like a second son and never made him pay. It was all good in the hood.

He grinned at the old pizza poster on the wall with the quote, *Pizza is a lot like sex. When it's good, it's really good. When it's bad, it's still pretty good.*

It was kind of Jhonny's family's motto.

Rosa muttered something under her breath and stomped

off to the kitchen.

"Why would she think I'd eat rancid chicken?" Ever looked bewildered.

Jhonny pondered the question as he surveyed the antique pizza pans and old pie signs dotting the walls. The comforting smell of homemade tomato sauce drifted out of the kitchen, making Jhonny's belly rumble. If only the pizza lovers squeezed into jam-packed booths had any idea her secret ingredient to her sauce was . . . sugar.

His sister came out of the kitchen. Vassena was two years younger and, his mother never failed to remind him, a lot more mature than Jhonny. After making a mistake on his birth certificate, the fact that Jhonny became a name nobody forgot, his mother deliberately misspelled Vanessa's name on her birth certificate. Vassena had legally changed it to Vanessa after crippling childhood taunting, but to some of her family members, she was still Vassena.

One of the huge reasons Jhonny and Ever became friends so fast was that Ever hadn't realized Jhonny's name was a mistake. Ever's mom was Colombian, and Jhon was a common name there, so he'd kept the name with pride. Vassena discovered Vanessa was a common girl's name in Colombia and changed it. Now she didn't have the mad eye twitch that had accompanied so much of her middle school years.

"Here you go." Her smiles were all for Ever, who cheerfully returned them. Ever was smart. He'd told Jhonny he was kind to anybody who handled his food because he'd seen first-hand what a pissed-off kitchen hand could do to a plate of innocent eats.

"Thanks, Vanessa." Ever always called her Vanessa, even when she wasn't around. Jhonny had started doing it, too. He didn't like the idea of her spitting on his food in the kitchen. Or doing worse. He watched the deft way she popped the gigantic pizza tray onto a wrought-iron tripod on the table, lighting the candle beneath it to keep the pie warm.

She was attractive, with the same chestnut brown hair that Jhonny had. Same big brown eyes, except she looked like she *ate* pizza for a living. As pretty as she was, her extra heft kept her single in a city that prized thinness. She'd met a few guys who liked pizza, but it always ended. Surprisingly, she took a lot of the idiots back . . . until she realized they really wanted free pizza, not a chubby girlfriend.

Vanessa slid a spatula under a couple of slices and popped them onto plates, depositing them in front of them. She arranged a small tray containing portions of red chili pepper flakes, freshly grated parmesan and fresh, chopped tomatoes. She topped it all off with a big smile. She was a kitchen superstar wizard, for sure.

"Enjoy," she said.

Both men thanked her, ogling the bubbling cheese on the restaurant's trademark square-shaped pie.

"You smell weird," she suddenly told Ever, before turning on her heel and heading back to the kitchen.

"And people wonder why she's still single," Ever deadpanned.

Jhonny laughed. Ever's cell phone rang as he bit into his gooey slice. He checked the readout.

"Lemme guess," Jhonny said, between bites. "Loverboy?"

Ever winced. "Don't call him that."

"You gonna tell me how he really weaseled a date out of you?"

"I told you already. I wanna see dead people." Ever helped himself to a second slice. "It was that or him calling the cops."

"Dude." Jhonny shook his head. They'd always managed to outrun Chris Coelho, the charm school dropout, in the past. Jhonny began to wonder if maybe Ever actually liked the guy.

"He's not so bad looking. I figure I could always shake him off at the exhibit if he's real snarky." Ever chewed thoughtfully. "Maybe he's just an ass on the job."

"You know he's an ass. Period." They'd met Coelho socially through their dweeb friends who, like Ever and Jhonny, prized old movies. They held monthly movie and popcorn nights at an old theater on Sunset. They always managed to find a couple of old stars from the movies to talk to the crowd. The old-time movie stars craved the attention. Ever and Jhonny also ran off ten-by-eight black-and-white photos for the stars to sign as part of the ticket price. They found copies of DVDs and videos of the movies to sell. Those screenings kept Ever and Jhonny afloat financially.

Two years ago, Ever had sold his share of a tour guide business that had started to fail the second he sold out to his ex-lover, Addison. It had broken Ever's heart to sell, but the two men hadn't been able to work together once their relationship ended. Jhonny quit pushing Ever on the subject of Coelho. If Ever was showing even the slightest interest in a living, breathing man, he should cut him some slack.

"I figure I'll meet him there," Ever said, as though he could read Jhonny's thoughts. "That way I can escape."

"Careful. He strikes me as being the vengeful type."

Ever sighed. "Yeah. I promised him we'd meet for lunch. There's some place he wants to go to near the exhibit."

"Where is the exhibit?"

"The California Science Center at Elysian Park. He wants to go to some Cuban restaurant."

"That sounds okay." Jhonny tried to act enthusiastic. Anything that involved a public meeting and Ever not winding up in the guy's apartment . . . or . . . dungeon . . . *stop it!* . . . was a good thing.

Ever nodded. There was a time when the two best friends

had explored some shared passion but couldn't find it. It even felt vaguely incestuous. As they told everyone they knew, they liked each other too much to screw up a good friendship.

When Jhonny's regular day job as a movie gaffer failed to produce work, he was grateful that Ever had introduced him to the world of writing and making a living via unorthodox methods. Now he dreaded the days when his union got him work. He loved the actual job of lighting a movie or TV set, but he hated the long hours, the whiny actors and the low pay for sixteen or seventeen hour days.

"I've been thinking."

"I'll let TMZ know," Ever joked.

Jhonny leaned his elbows on the table, hoping his mom didn't see him. Even at his age of twenty-nine, she still thought it was okay to discipline him with a slap here and there.

"No. Seriously, I have."

"Should I be scared?" Ever smiled at him.

"No. Well . . . maybe just a bit." He took a deep breath. "Your exclusivity, non-competitive clause in your contract with Steve is up. Or just about up . . . and word has it on the gay gossip vine that little Stevie is going under. I was thinking . . . what if we open a museum and operate a tour out of it? We could do a walking tour of Old Hollywood . . . couple of bus tours . . . even a Hollywood Ghost Tour on Saturday nights."

Ever dropped the slice he'd been munching and sat back in his booth, staring at him. He gulped his soda, then wiped his fingers with a paper napkin. He was about to speak when Jhonny's mom stopped and snatched up their soda glasses.

"Refills?" she asked, racing off without waiting for a reply.

Ever said nothing until she returned with their drinks.

"I think that's an amazing idea," he said. "I've got six months to go on the contract, but"—he leaned forward, his voice dropping—"I've heard the reports, too. Steve *is* going under. I'd kinda like to buy the business back from him, but he'd never sell to me."

Jhonny pointed a finger at him. "Exactly. Which is why I've been thinking. We can open a museum, or at least work on finding a good location for one, start getting it ready and maybe induce some people we know to help buy the business back from Addison."

"I like that idea. Like a conglomerate."

Jhonny nodded. "Then we open the museum, and we fold the tour business into it. It really grills my cheese that you started that company, and you had to just . . . hand it over to that lying, cheating, pole-dancing bastard."

Ever smiled at him. "Thanks, bro. Though technically speaking, he didn't do much pole-dancing. He just gave all our money to twinks that do."

Jhonny knew that Ever was a loyal and loving guy when he fell for a man. He'd been devastated when he'd discovered Addison's slutty ways.

He kept his tone gentle. "If he won't sell to us, we wait out the six months and start up a different business, like what I just said."

"It sounds good to me. I love the whole idea . . . and, of course, I'd like to get my business back. I have no idea what he'd want for it. Or even who would have money to invest."

"We know a ton of people," Jhonny said. "Now I know you're interested, I'll sniff around."

Ever pointed to the last piece of pizza on the tray. "Just for that, you get the last slice."

"Just for that, I'll take it."

Jhonny slid the still-warm pie off, watching Ever cover

the warming candle with its metal cap.

"Something weird's been happening," Ever blurted. "I keep dreaming about a guy on a motorcycle. I hear motorcycles everywhere. I don't even like motorcycles."

"Is it a guy you know?" Jhonny asked.

"No. But he knows me. And he doesn't speak English. But he keeps talking. He's like a male Chatty Cathy. I even hear motorcycles when I'm driving. I look around. Nothing. Do you think I'm losing my mind?"

Before Johnny could respond, his mom skidded to a stop beside them. "Finished?" She sometimes reminded Jhonny of the housekeeper, Alice, in the old *Brady Bunch* series, especially since she'd taken to wearing hospital-style footwear. She had a new lease on life in her ergonomically sound shoes.

"Dessert?" Again she took off before they could answer. She returned with huge chunks of tiramisu and two cups of coffee.

"Lunch is on the house," she announced.

"Thank you," the two men chorused. "Except . . ." Rosa eyed Ever in a predatory way. "I told Vassena you'd take her to the movies with her friends on Saturday night."

"I keep telling you I'm gay," he told her.

"No, you're not. You just haven't met the right woman yet."

Jhonny groaned.

Rosa warmed up her theme a little more. "You want a nice, healthy, robust woman who can cook. You want a woman who knows how to sizzle in the kitchen, and in the bedroom if you know what I mean." She tapped the framed pizza-is-sex sign for extra emphasis.

"Mom!" Jhonny bleated.

Ever stared up at her. "What movie?"

"*Mission Impossible.* She has tickets to that fancy-schmancy

Bridge Theater. You know, the one with reclining seats and table service. The whole night is on me."

"All right," Ever said. As Jhonny's mom drifted away on her happy cloud, Ever leaned into him again across the table.

"Next time, I'll insist she brings us the check. That's two duty dates I've got in one week."

"Being a nice guy blows monkey chunks don't it?" Jhonny grinned, tucking into his tiramisu.

CHAPTER TWO

"My idea of the perfect date is pizza, champagne and a hot guy blowing me," Chris Coelho said a few minutes after he showed up to their lunch date the following day.

Ever shivered in spite of the warmth of their sunny meeting spot by the fountain in Elysian Park.

That's never going to happen. Ever felt the color rising up his throat and face. How embarrassing. Chris had just loudly revealed his gay status in a very gay-unfriendly section of town. On top of that, he'd showed up in a security guard uniform, freaking out a lot of the families picnicking on the grass. Most were hard-working illegal immigrants who couldn't tell a security guard from a cop. As they scrambled to gather their things and flee, Chris seemed oblivious to the frantic parents and wailing babies as he swaggered across the grass like a cut-rate *RoboCop*.

To add insult to injury, he'd also come without his wallet.

"I left it at home," he said, his tone breezy. "You mind lending me a couple of bucks for gas later?"

Ever mentally rolled his eyes and gave him a fiver. As money changed hands the roar of a motorcycle made Ever jump. He looked around. *Nothing.*

Chris palmed the note, leering at him. "So, since you're playing hard to get, I'll settle for Cuban chicken . . . for now."

Ever cringed at Chris's words and manic smirk. The so-called Cuban place that the guy raved about turned out to be

18

one of the ubiquitous food trucks that had popped up all over LA. Since Chris was paying for the tickets to the Mummy exhibit, Ever decided to be a good sport and spring for lunch.

As they waited for their food, he reasoned that at least he wouldn't feel so guilty now if he wanted to make a fast getaway from the museum.

"By the way, I don't have tickets," Chris announced as they sat on the grass with Styrofoam containers.

"You don't?" Ever's heart sank. Tickets were expensive and, he knew, the exhibit's entire last, extended week was sold out. *What a cluster fuck, dammit.* He really wanted to see this show.

"I'm gonna sneak you in there. I'm working the museum today. Nobody will question it."

"You're going to sneak me in?"

"Yeah . . . easy peasy. Say, you're still limping. Guess I was kinda rough on you when I took you down yesterday." Chris grinned. "Sometimes I don't know my own strength, but you did run from me, dude. I bet you're a real tiger in the sack, Ever."

He leaned into Ever growling, "Grrrr . . . grrrf!"

Ever wanted to barf. He edged away from Chris, concerned about getting into the museum.

"Are you sure this is a good idea?" Ever's heart sank. He wanted to see the mummies. He was all about mummies.

"Don't be silly. It's fine. Besides, we have a deal, right?"

Right. But still Ever hesitated. His foot felt a lot better than it had the day before, but what if he had to get out of the place in a hurry? He started to worry about how his foot would hold up over a long museum trek or being chased by a sneering Chris Coelho, not to mention the fact that he didn't actually have a damned ticket. What if another security guard asked him for proof of it? This was the hottest museum show in town. Over a million people so far had attended it.

Chris shrugged off such a suggestion. "I'll be there. Don't you worry. I won't let anyone haul my man off to the pokey. You gonna eat those plantains?"

Ever's smile froze. *My . . . man?* He shoved his plantains toward Coelho. This was shaping up to be the date from hell.

Coelho was so in love with his rent-a-cop status he boasted about arrests and takedowns on the studio lot that made the place sound like the OK Corral, not a sleepy studio backlot. He mentioned he also worked at the Petersen Museum — home to a bunch of rare automobiles and had, according to Chris, foiled several attempts at grand theft auto.

The stories grew more and more outlandish, Chris mistaking Ever's numb silence for rapt attention.

If he's working the exhibit today, then he won't be with me the whole time. As soon as I can, I'll get the fuck outta there.

They walked over to the Science Center, but Chris dragged him away from the throng congregating in the long line out front.

"I'm taking you in through the security entrance."

"Are you joking?" Ever had a fleeting, wild thought that Chris might be trying to set him up.

"Hell, no." Coelho looked so pleased with himself. "I knew you'd be happy."

He'd obviously misunderstood Ever's expression of horror and thought his date was happy. *Happy!*

They entered the museum via the rear doors. The whole place was dark once they got inside. The musty smell didn't help when Chris's hand landed on the small of his back. The gesture didn't comfort him. On the contrary, it felt like tendrils of ice spiking up and down his back. Coelho's mouth moved over his in a stealthy, snake-like kiss.

Eeew!

"Hey," a voice said in the darkness. "Cut that out."

Another guard approached them, waving a flashlight around. "We're having trouble with the lights. This is your boyfriend?" He focused the light on Ever's face, blinding him for a moment.

"Yeah." Chris kept his arm around Ever in a territorial way as they followed the second guy along a dark passage.

"You're right, dude. He's hot." The guard grinned over the arc of light, motioning them to follow.

My God, I'm breaking into the hottest exhibit in town like a goddamn thief. Say . . . this is amazing.

Ever soon forgot his qualms as they spilled out into the museum from one of the emergency exits. He blinked, his eyes adjusting to the bright light. His gaze roamed the room as case after case revealed startling mummies. He hadn't expected to see animals . . . there were cats, dogs, a baboon, even a monkey in an elaborate feathered costume. He didn't know where to start.

"I was like that the first time I came in here, too," Chris said, smiling. "Here's a program. I stashed it for you."

"Thank you." For a moment, Ever felt giddy with the pleasure and power of having the exhibit to himself. It was an amazing feeling. He'd come here for other exhibits and had to take photos over the heads of dozens of other people.

The one hundred fifty mummies came from all over the world, not just Egypt. Ever was surprised to see so many European mummies, especially from England and Germany. The Hungarian couple and their perfectly preserved son tore at his heart. They had all died together in the eighteenth century, and their bodies had been found in an old church. The thirteenth-century tattooed woman from Peru intrigued him. He soon forgot about his crummy date as he read the information about each of the mummies.

One of the oldest was a Peruvian baby who pre-dated King Tut. There was also a seventeenth-century German nobleman, whose mummified body had been found in his family's castle. Scientists hypothesized that he had remained in such good condition because the castle's walls had been sealed, keeping the body dry. Now that body was traveling the world with mummified lizards and an embryonic baby that had died due to a rare spinal deformity.

The Science Center opened up to the public at large. He heard the babble of voices as he stared down at the Egyptian mummy lying in a long, flat glass display case. His attention returned to the tattooed woman, sitting up. The printed information indicated she'd suffered from arthritis in her hands and back. She had been forty-five or fifty when she died.

He wanted to know more. Had she been in agony at the end? Her long brown hair fanned over her shoulders, her head tilted at an odd angle.

Ever moved on to the sarcophagus of an Egyptian priest called Nes-Pa-Qa-Shuti. It dated back to 650 BC. Ever stared at the ornate funeral container . . . a sharp contrast with the Egyptian mummy from 408 BC. He lay unadorned, his head raised as if he wanted to leap from the glass case. Ever had the odd feeling the mummy had the urge to escape so many people staring at him. Ever felt sorry for the guy. He seemed naked next to the priest in the sarcophagus. Ever's gaze moved over to the mummified dog. He felt a cold hand on his ass and turned to snap at Chris, only he wasn't there.

Turning around Ever didn't see anyone close. Tons of people swirled around him. A shiver ran through him.

I'm just imagining things. Nobody touched me.

He turned to stare at the Egyptian mummies once more and felt the chilly sensation of cold fingers on his butt again. This time he jumped. He quickly turned and saw Chris walking away from him.

Okay, he's a jerk. Next time I'll say something.

Ever walked from one case to the next, riveted by the

skinny, standing dog in one of the cases. As he studied it, he became aware of Chris leering at him from the other side of the glass.

Oh, brother.

"What do you think?" Chris asked.

"I think it's amazing."

Chris pointed to the Hungarian mummy's elaborate, blue velvet burial outfit.

"I wouldn't be caught dead in that. Get it? Ha ha!"

Ever struggled to find a smile for the guy.

"I finish in a couple of hours. Why don't you hang out and wait for me . . . we can go finish what we started." He made a kissing sound.

A loud bang up front sent Chris running. It gave Ever the chance he needed. He made a dash for it to the nearest emergency exit.

Jhonny watched the realtor struggle with the keylock on the aged storefront door. He'd offered twice to give it a try, but she was determined to do it herself.

"I need to do it so I can show the next prospective buyer around," she said.

He took the extra moments to look up and down Hollywood Boulevard. Wall to wall Hollywood museums right along the same few blocks. There was no one big, definitive Hollywood Museum. Just a bunch of smaller ones. He could see the gaudy sign for Madame Tussaud's Hollywood Wax Museum, the new kid on the block right next to Grauman's Chinese Theater.

That, too, was fairly new. Grauman's had been renamed Mann's for decades until a recent sentimental push restored the original name. The theater itself was spectacular and housed a hundred years of celebrity footprints. Tussaud's had replaced the old and awful Movieland Museum. Tussaud's was a respected name in wax museums all over the world—the Hollywood version to Jhonny's mind was just meh.

Tussaud's had done away with Movieland's elaborate stage settings for their wax figures and the horrible alarms if you got to close to them, but he didn't think the wax celebrities themselves did their live counterparts justice. They weren't as bad as the Hollywood Wax Museum, where some of the wax models needed urgent repairs. Some of them had clouded eyes and bad wigs. They were embarrassing.

Along the same block was the Ripley's Believe it Or Not Museum, and now housed in the old Max Factor building on the corner of Highland was the Hollywood Museum. There, you could see all kind of movie props and costumes. They had W.C. Fields's trademark top hat, Sylvester Stallone's *Rocky* boxing gloves, silent screen legend Mary Pickford's blonde curls, Errol Flynn's dueling pistols from *Against All Flags,* and other interesting bits and pieces.

There were a few other museums scattered around, including the Gene Autry Western Museum over in Griffith Park . . . but was there room for one more Hollywood history museum?

"Gotcha!"

The realtor's excited voice stomped on his thoughts as she rolled up the metal garage door over the storefront window. He peered inside, staggered to see the array of ancient mannequins lining the window. Some still stood, a couple of them had fallen, their graceful arms reaching up toward nothingness. They reminded him of mummies. It spooked him just a little.

"How long did you say the building's been closed?" he asked.

"Two years. The property's been in litigation tied up in

probate court." She opened the door from a key in her pocket. "You may have read about it. The owner was murdered."

He shook his head. "No, I don't recall. Who was the
owner?"

"Well, you're going to have to find out anyway. State law.
Full disclosure." She pushed at the heavy glass door, a
strange odor wafting out as the door finally gave.

Jhonny knew the smell. Rats. So many of these old build-
ings had them.

He followed her inside. The realtor, Janet Margew, was a
regular at Crazy Pie. She'd just received the listing and, as a
favor to Jhonny's mom, had let him come look at it before
she even printed out a listing sheet or prepared it for online
viewing. God he wished Ever could be here to see it. As if on
cue, his cell phone rang. He was ecstatic to see it was Ever.
He took the call.

"How's it going?"

"The exhibit was amazing, and the date's going fan-
tabulously now I'm outta there." Ever chuckled. "What are
you doing? I see you called a couple of times."

"Dude. You gotta come over here. I think I found us a
museum space."

"Already? Where?"

"Heart of Hollywood, baby. It's the old Benkman Fur
Salon."

"Oh, yeah ... I remember reading about that. The wife
had the husband murdered."

Jhonny found himself smiling. Ever sure knew his Hollywood history.

"I'll be there in ten minutes," he said.

Ever made it in just under eight minutes. Janet took a lik-
ing to him straight away. Women always liked Ever. They
always wanted to convert him. He was handsome in a
heartbreaking way. He always seemed oblivious to people

noticing him—men or women.

Jhonny watched Ever take it all in. The space was surprisingly huge, with two floors, a small stage that must have been used to model furs. There was a kitchen in back, a bathroom, and even a handicapped entrance. All of these were now state-mandated.

"We can use these mannequins for some of our costume displays," Ever said. "Man, it's in great shape, isn't it?"

Jhonny nodded. It was a find. A real find.

"How much?" Ever asked.

The realtor smiled. "The family has been embroiled in the court case over the estate. Their real concern was the furs since most of them were vintage. The salon . . . well, they're willing to let it go, but there are some bills owing on it." She passed Ever the bank's printout that detailed the account transactions. Storage fees, state and city fines. It went on and on. Jhonny tried not to feel offended that she'd bypassed him in favor of Ever.

Ever, however, held the paper so they could both read it, then passed it straight over to Jhonny.

"What do you think?" Ever asked.

"I love it." Jhonny held his breath. This was their museum. He was certain of it. He watched his best friend wander over to the grimy windows and peer outside.

"It feels right," Ever finally said.

"Feels right to me, too."

The two friends stared at one another.

"We need to jump on this," Ever said. "What kind of deposit do you need?"

"I need to start with a credit check." Janet became all business. Jhonny didn't care. He hadn't seen that gleam in his best friend's eyes for a long, long time. The fun-loving little boy inside Ever was back in town.

Ever and Jhonny sat at their kitchen table, a yellow, Formica-topped prop from one of *The Partridge Family* shows. Ever had his laptop open, and as Jhonny made handwritten notes to himself, Ever typed in the list of names of people they knew who had money and would be likely to invest in their big adventure.

"I don't know anyone we can put the bite on, quite frankly." Ever leaned back in his chair. That was a relic from *I Love Lucy*, along with their living room sofa. They looked after their furniture lovingly and occasionally let people into their home to see their amazing collection.

"You can't ask your mom?" Jhonny asked.

"No, but I could ask my aunt." He pondered the issue. It still rankled with him that his mom had maintained close ties with his ex-lover, Addison. In fact, they had remained so close she'd invited Addison to her annual Thanksgiving feast and suggested Ever might want to skip their traditional family meal. Yeah, that hurt a bunch. His mom would probably invest in the new business since she'd done well in the past out of her son, not only getting back her initial investment but a tidy interest as well. The fact was, he couldn't trust her not to tell Addison.

He voiced his thoughts aloud, and Jhonny nodded. "You think we can ask Xenia? Won't she feel compelled to tell your mom?"

"God . . . I don't . . . well . . . dang. Now I think about it, I really don't know."

"Let me ask around. I have a couple of ideas."

Ever smiled. "Cool."

The two roommates went over plans and ideas, turning their attention at last to their latest acquisition, the spaceship.

"Guess I should clean it up some more," Jhonny said with

a sigh. "That smell of chicken isn't getting any better."

Ever laughed. His clothes had stunk the day before. He'd washed them twice and dried them with tons of dryer sheets.

"I may never eat chicken again," he joked.

Their house phone rang.

"It's my dad." Jhonny pulled a face.

Ever checked his watch. "I guess it's time," he said.

Jhonny groaned. "Yeah. It's time."

"It's only five hours," Ever reminded him.

"That's true . . . and I can use the time to butter him up . . . maybe he'll invest in the business."

Ever nodded. Jhonny's parents were happily married — up to a point. His father had grown tired of pizza and opened a retro bowling alley a few blocks from Crazy Pie. It had turned out to be a great idea since bowling customers could order pizza and pasta and have it delivered right to their bowling lanes. Three evenings a week, Jhonny and Ever worked the front desk for league nights when every professional bowler in the valley came in for their competition games.

As Jhonny answered the phone and assured his father they were on their way, Ever thought about how aggressive bowlers could be. Underneath their unfashionable clothes lurked often hostile personalities. On league nights, things often came to blows and security guards intervened.

Ever grimaced. *Security guards . . .* that meant Chris Coelho would be in the house. He was part of the group of security guard friends that moonlighted at the bowling alley. Ugh. Ever hadn't heard from him since he'd run off earlier in the day. Maybe Chris hadn't noticed or . . . hadn't cared. That brightened his mood, just thinking that Chris might not be a problem.

On the plus side, Jhonny would get a chance to ogle his

new crush. He had a mad thing for a new security guard and wannabe actor, Mike Fletcher. Ever personally thought the blond bombshell was more of a conceited bubblehead. The guy was so vain Ever had caught him staring at himself in mirrors around the bowling alley. In fact, he'd spotted him getting an eyeful in any shiny surface . . . like his own, well-polished bowling ball. Mike was a bowling fanatic.

Jhonny brushed his teeth and hair, a smile on his face.

"Wonder if Mike will be there?" he asked. He seemed to be making hard work of his neutral tone.

"Sure he will," Ever said. "I've seen the way he looks at you."

Jhonny perked. Ever wasn't being kind. He was being honest. He wondered how long it would take Mike to hit on Jhonny, because Jhonny's painful shyness guaranteed they'd be reduced to merely grinning at each other for the rest of their lives.

The two friends jumped into Jhonny's car and headed up to Gallo Lanes, chitchatting about the new business. It started to rain. Ever knew this meant a busy night. People would want to hunker down someplace warm and dry, with damned good pizza.

"Holy shit." Jhonny slapped his dashboard as they waited at a red light.

"What is it?" Ever asked, leaning forward to follow Jhonny's gaze through the river of water bucketing the windshield.

"My fucking window wipers got stolen, dude."

For some reason that struck Ever as pathetic and hysterical at the same time, even though it was dangerous as hell to be driving in the rain without them.

"It could only happen to you."

"Yeah. Lucky me." Jhonny growled as they drove slowly, his head hanging out of the window. He pulled in the bowling alley's parking lot, almost running down his father.

"Hey, dickhead!" Jimmy Gallo shouted, shaking his fist at his son. "You on drugs?"

"Not my fault!" Jhonny screamed, winding down the window. "I got no window wipers, and I can't see a damned thing!"

Once inside, Ever was surprised to see Chris walking around in aimless circles. He seemed to be studying the carpet pattern. How weird. He looked up, a gleam of recognition in his eyes then dropped his head again.

"What's up with your boyfriend?" Jhonny asked.

"He's not my boyfriend," Ever snapped, sotto.

"Whatever. He's acting real weird," Jhonny said. "Even for him. What the hell's he lookin' at?"

"Been like this ever since I saw him on the street," Jhonny's father told them. "He was just sauntering along . . . one of the other guards dropped him off apparently. I picked him up, and he kept laughing."

"Laughing?" Ever seemed startled.

"Yeah. He kept playing with the damned radio like he'd never seen one in his whole life. What the fuck is he doing now?"

They all looked over in the direction of his pointed finger. Chris stood at a party table, head down, sniffing a huge pizza with great suspicion.

"If he doesn't get his nose out of that damned pie I'll have to chuck it," Jimmy grumbled. He raced over to Chris, waving the guy away like a pesky bug. Jimmy Gallo had the same good looks as his son, but a massive middle. Now that Ever thought about it, he kinda looked like a bowling pin.

Chris shrugged and went back to his examination of the carpet. Ever watched him, a little worried. Chris was acting really strange. Guilt overcame him, and he walked over, tapping him on the shoulder. Chris glanced up, a bewildered look on his face. He grabbed Ever's shirt collar, whispering in his ear dramatically.

"The floor is . . . dirty."

Ever cocked a brow. "No shit, Sherlock. I doubt it's ever been cleaned." He glanced around in panic. "Don't tell Waldo I said that, but he's probably the worst cleaner in town."

Chris's attention had shifted to the teams of bowlers that had just arrived, in their uniform color shirts, lucky shoes and bowling balls in hand.

He seemed even more befuddled now. "Which one cleans the floor?"

Ever ignored the bizarre question and hastened behind the counter before Mr. Gallo could bawl him out. He and Jhonny had a busy half hour organizing the players. Jhonny always left the difficult pairings to Ever because he could never remember which players hated each other and which players had restraining orders against each other thanks to two recently collapsed marriages on account of infidelity.

For a bunch of people into such a boring, old-fashioned sport, Ever never could get over what a raunchy crowd they were.

There were six teams that refused to play near one another on account of bad feelings and, apparently, bad luck associated with bowling too close to one another as a result. With the teams finally assembled in their lanes, Jhonny and Ever made sure all the equipment was working and that the electronic scoring system was on line. Though Gallo Lanes had a retro feel to it, the electronic scoring was modern. It saved a lot of bad blood and made for more drinking time for the players.

Chris stood in the middle of one of the lanes, his toes on the brink of the foul line, staring up at an illuminated scoring pad on the wall above the team's scoring table.

"He's staring at it like he's never seen it before. What the hell do you think he's been smoking?" Jhonny mused. He glanced at Ever. "Wonder if it's Maui Wowie. I've never seen him so goofy, or so . . . pleasant."

"No idea. But he's in Rambo's lane. He's not picking up his cell phone calls. I'm gonna hafta go and get him out of there."

Franklin Rambo was the most difficult man on the bowling circuit. He was middle-aged and unattractive, but with a name like Rambo, he thought it gave him some kind of movie star cache. He wielded his unpleasant personality around like a samurai sword.

"Move it, pal," Rambo grumbled at Chris, who ran to watch in fascination as a bowling ball shot up from the motorized chute at the lane beside them.

"Sorry," Ever said, pulling Chris away. Rambo gave him a sour look. Ever bit the inside of his cheek to keep from laughing. Rambo had dressed in his trademark khaki pants and brown sweater. He had pulled his giant, grandpa-white underpants up and over the sweater and the waistband poked out above his pants and belt. He looked like a moron.

"What the heck is going on with you?" Ever asked Chris as the music came on over the sound system.

Chris brightened. "Radio!"

Ever stared at him. Chris didn't even sound like himself. His voice was deeper and more modulated.

"Are you all right, Chris?"

"Chris." Chris had that befuddled look again.

"Ever!" Jhonny screamed at him. Ever raced over to the front desk. "I'm run off my feet here!"

"Sorry," Ever said again. When he turned to check on Chris, the guy had vanished. *Whatever.* He got back behind the counter and didn't have time to even think about Chris until he heard shouts and laughter coming from one of the lanes several minutes later.

Dear God. Everyone had stopped bowling. They were all staring at Chris, who was running down one of the bowling lanes. Of course, it had to be Rambo's lane again, worse luck. Rambo paced the edge of the foul line yelling at Chris to come back. Easier said than done. The incredibly slick surface had turned Chris's attempts to get out of it into a desperate fight to stay on his feet. He skidded and slipped, tumbling into the gutter lane, sliding down flat on his back. One foot smashed into the ten pins waiting to be hit by a ball—not somebody's feet. The automatic pin gate came down to clear away the pins, Chris wrenching his leg away just in time.

Franklin Rambo stood, hands on hips, watching Chris's peculiar performance. The only sound now was Elvis Presley warbling 'The Edge of Reality' over the sound system. How apt.

Jhonny nudged Ever. "Congratulations. Your boyfriend is a real head case."

"He's not my boyfriend."

"Yeah . . . .right. I've seen the way you keep looking at him."

"I'm worried about him. He's acting . . . well . . . you can see it. Strange."

"Strange for him or strange for anybody?"

"Certifiable." Ever saw the longing look Jhonny slid toward Mike Fletcher, who was busy pacing the area by the party table. Ever's glance shifted back to Rambo's lane. His heart sank when he saw the sly smile creep across Rambo's face as he turned, grinning at the crowd. He sauntered to the bowling ball roundabout next to the chute. He casually took his ball out and slowly approached the lane as Chris still fought to get to his feet. His clothes looked greasy from the oiled wood surface, and the panic on his face was heart-wrenching.

Ever had no idea why he felt the need to protect Chris from what was certainly going to be a brutal knockdown via Franklin Rambo's blood red Ebonite Mission 2.0 custom-made bowling ball. Some deep inner instinct, however, sent him scuttling around the counter to the lane, screaming.

"Stop!" He waved his arms.

The crowd turned as one, staring at him.

"Don't get involved!" Jhonny yelled, but it was too late. Ever reached the foul line and slipped. He fell right across it, landing on his ass, everybody laughing at him. Chris tottered toward him as if he was an overgrown child just learning to walk.

Ever got to his feet, the crowd roaring now.

"Hit him! Hit him!" they began to chant.

Huh?

Too late, Ever heard the *whoosh* and *thunk* of Rambo's ball aiming right at him. He tried to outrun it, but it clipped his left heel, sending him hard to his knees, sliding all the way into Chris's legs. Chris fell on his back, his head bouncing a couple of times on the floor. Ever came to a stop right between Chris's thighs, his face buried in the man's crotch. His already injured leg was wedged uncomfortably at an awkward angle. He felt old and heavy and—oh, no, another bowling ball was coming right at them.

Chris reached for him, pulling him to safety, the second ball just missing Ever by a fraction of an inch. It smashed into the pin gate, which had come down. It hit so hard, it dented the gate and started rolling back toward them.

From somewhere in the crowd, somebody shouted, "Strike!"

"Gutterballs!" somebody else yelled making everyone laugh louder.

The emergency lane alarm sounded.

A staff technician raced over to Ever and Chris along the wooden strip between lanes. "What the fuck?" he yelled.

Ever stopped the rolling ball, pushing it toward the gutter with his shoulder. With the big, burly technician's help, he got to his feet, more embarrassed than injured.

"Don't worry about me, I'm worried about him." Ever jutted his chin toward Chris, who wasn't moving. His eyes lay open, but he seemed someplace else. He suddenly raised his head as the technician knelt beside him. Ever tried to remember the guy's name, but they'd only met once in passing.

"Where am I? What the fuck am I doing flat on my back here?"

"Easy, easy," the technician said.

"But . . . how did I get here?"

"We'll help you," Ever said, but began slipping again.

"Walk back thataway." The technician pointed to the narrow, wooden strip between Rambo's gutter lane and the one beside it. Ever walked slowly, taking his time, but the show was apparently over. Somebody had broken out fresh pizza and beer. Everybody stampeded for the party tables. All except Rambo, who stood at the foul line and sneered.

"Having fun?" he asked. "You ruined my game."

"And you tried to kill me when I was trying to help a fellow employee."

"Don't be so dramatic. You looked nice and cozy out there."

"Yeah?" Ever longed to punch the guy in the eye. "Whatever, dude."

He turned and saw the technician helping Chris down the lane. They were taking a long time.

"Asshole," Rambo muttered.

"Yeah, you really are," Ever responded and blew right past him.

"What happened to me?" Chris whined when he caught up with Ever. "What the fuck happened tonight?"

"Don't you know?"

Chris stared at him. "Man, my head hurts." He put a hand to the back of his scalp. I got a big ol' lump back there. We got any ice?"

"I'll get you some," Jhonny said. He beckoned Ever to the desk. "Can you take over for a few? I'm gonna go to the ice machine. Mike disappeared. Have you seen him?"

"No, dude. I was busy getting knocked down by bowling balls."

"I told you not to get involved. Oh, shit. Here comes Rambo."

Jhonny took off, leaving Ever to deal with the king of all bullshit.

"Where's the owner? I wanna complain," Rambo said.

"Did you fucking throw a bowling ball at us?" Chris interrupted. "You could have killed us."

"You were in my lane."

The technician who'd rescued Ever and Chris came up to them. Chris's entire demeanor changed.

"Why don't you like me?" he asked Rambo, his lip quivering. Aw geez . . . was the big bad security guard going to cry?

"What?" Rambo looked nonplussed.

"Concussion," Ever said. "He hit the lane pretty hard. I'm sure it was all caught on tape."

"Tape?" Rambo's eyes widened.

"Yeah." Ever pointed to the security cameras. "I think I'm getting some whiplash. I'd love my lawyer to see that footage."

"Fuck you," Rambo grumbled and would have stalked off, except that Chris let loose with some weird karate chop to the guy's neck that dropped him.

He stumbled a couple of feet and fell with a hard plop to the carpet, swaying on his knees before keeling over, flat on his face. People milled around him.

Ever noticed nobody rushed to his aid.

"Think he's dead?" one woman asked.

"No." Ever knelt and checked Rambo's pulse.

"What a shame," she said and walked off.

"They really tape this shit?" the technician asked, glancing up at the camera.

"No," Ever said. "They're stage props."

"Oh, in that case . . ." He gave Rambo the finger and trudged away from the desk.

"Help me." Ever nudged Chris and knelt beside the sprawled Rambo whose open mouth drooled all over the carpet. Ever glanced up, but Chris was now mesmerized by the lineup of credit card machines on the desk.

"What the fuck's going on?" Jhonny asked, coming around the corner.

"Help me, will you?" Ever begged.

"Oh, my God. Do we need to call an ambulance?" Jhonny looked worried.

Rambo had awakened and kept blinking his eyes. They propped him against the desk as he blinked and smacked his lips together, glancing around.

"What the . . ."

"Are you okay?" Jhonny asked.

Rambo's face was a dangerous shade of red. "Think I'm gonna puke," Rambo muttered and got to his feet, hurrying past them.

"Radio?" Chris kept bleating at the rack of credit cards machines on the counter, pressing numbers and putting his ear to each one.

"What the fuck?" Jhonny pointed at Chris as a loud retching sound reached their ears. "Oh, fuckin' A." Jhonny raced over to where Rambo knelt on the carpet, an inch from the men's room entrance, hurling his guts out.

Chris joined them just as Mike Fletcher emerged from the men's room, zipping up his fly. He was accompanied by an older, balding guy who was wiping off his mouth with the back of his hand. Ever, hard on Jhonny's heels, didn't know who he felt worse for. Jhonny, whose hot crush had been toilet trading with one of the middle-aged bowlers, or Rambo, who was barfing in public.

"I feel better now," Rambo announced and stumbled back to his game.

"Glad someone does." Jhonny looked devastated.

"I'll clean this up," Ever offered, though the stench of puke made him feel sick.

Mike stared at them all, apparently oblivious to the misery on Jhonny's face, and walked right around them, passing them by.

"What an ass," Ever said.

"Yeah." Jhonny's gaze fell. "This whole night has been too frickin' weird."

Ever caught a glimpse of Chris following Mike toward the bowling lanes, a mesmerized expression on his face.

"You think there's something in the water?" Ever asked Jhonny, who returned to the counter, a hopeless shrug his only response. Evan walked to the back room and found the cleaning crew starting to get organized.

"We had a barfing issue," he said, to Waldo, who headed the crew.

"Excellent," he deadpanned.

"I'll clean it up," Ever said. "You have anything I can use to get the mess off the floor?"

Waldo shook his head. "Only you would offer, Ever. Thanks, but no thanks. It's my job. Now, take me to ground zero."

He was a cute guy, that's for sure. Waldo cleaned the bowling alley with a rotating female crew, all sisters. Rumor had it he bonked them all, but Ever wondered if it were true. He never saw the women fight or argue, and Waldo smiled like life was too good somehow. *Well, dang.* Maybe he was dipping his wick with them all. Maybe he was so busy doing that he didn't have time to actually clean the joint.

Ever led Waldo back to the site.

"Nothing to it." Waldo spritzed the mess with a bottle of something that smelled pretty good, in spite of the awful smell of the carpet. "Leave it to me, Ever."

No problem. Ever returned to the counter where Mike tried to shake off Chris.

"What's with loony tunes here tonight?" Mike jabbed his thumb in Chris's direction. "He tried to kiss my feet, for chrissakes."

"He did?" Now Ever felt put out.

"Goddress." Chris kept reaching out a hand to Mike's blond locks.

"Cut that out, will ya?" Mike smacked his hand out of the way and stalked away.

"What, you don't want him to blow you in the john?" Ever asked his voice low.

Mike stopped in his tracks. He turned to say something, his gaze hooded as it shifted between Ever and Jhonny behind the counter.

"Goddress," Chris said again, his hand on Mike's hair. Mike slapped him away again and pushed off through the crowd.

"Royalty," Chris said. "He must be protected." He took off after him.

"He's a royal fuckwad is what he is." Jhonny sounded depressed. "Can you believe how weird this night has been?"

"No." Ever shook his head.

"Two hours to go. Unfrickinbelievable. Hopefully, it'll get

easier."

Jhonny spoke too soon. Ten seconds later the entire bowling alley plunged into darkness, punctuated by a woman's sharp, shrill scream.

CHAPTER THREE

Jhonny waited outside as the paramedics helped out the three men whose fight in Rambo's lane had resulted in a complete short-circuiting of the alley's electrical system. Though the building had its own generator, something had fried half the board. Nobody could explain it, not even the fire department Station 60 chief who said he'd never seen anything like it. The chief had shut down the whole facility until the Department of Water and Power could dispatch a crew first thing in the morning.

Mike, Rambo, and Chris had gotten into some kind of weird row over Mike's hair. Chris seemed obsessed with it. Poor Waldo had stepped in to defend Chris, who apparently had been trying to kiss Mike's feet again. Now Waldo was on a stretcher, insisting he was okay. Mike and Rambo seemed to be nursing hurt egos more than anything. Chris also seemed unscathed but sat staring into space on a soaked window box with bedraggled geraniums drowning inside it. What the hell was up with the guy?

The paramedics loaded up the truck with their hoses and stuff, Rambo and Waldo flipping each other off as they left. Jhonny watched Mike for a moment, trying not to think about the fact that the guy had let some married bowler blow him in the men's room.

Geez, I have a frickin' knack for falling for such losers. Yeah, another one bites the dust. Here I was thinking all this time that he was shy. Shy! Bastard just likes rush jobs.

Mike must have sensed Jhonny staring at him. He walked

over, lifting a hand.

"I'm okay, guy," he said.

"You sure?" Jhonny had to play it cool. Pissed as he was, the last thing he needed was his dad getting a bunch of lawsuits from his customers *and* his staff.

"Sure I'm sure. And listen, I can explain about the old guy sucking my cock. It wasn't my idea."

Jhonny was so surprised Mike mentioned it that it triggered a flash of fury deep inside him.

"It was an accident?" The whole evening pissed off Jhonny more than he cared to admit. He couldn't help the scornful tone.

"Not an accident . . . no. But it *was* a mistake." Mike rubbed his head and stepped forward an inch. "Fuck . . . I'm pretty banged up."

Jhonny said nothing.

"Listen . . . I was taking a leak, and he was standing next to me . . . next thing I knew he was stroking me. I couldn't believe it."

Jhonny stared at him.

"He wasn't hot . . . or anything like that, but damn, Jhonny, it wasn't his first time, if you know what I mean. He got me all worked up in no time."

Jhonny shook his head. "Man, nothing like that ever happens to me."

Mike shrugged. "Me either . . . until tonight. I gotta admit having some guy begging you to let him suck your cock beats just about anything."

"I guess." Jhonny wasn't sure if he felt better or worse hearing these details. "Weren't you afraid you were gonna get caught?" He couldn't resist asking.

"Kinda . . . um . . . a thrill actually. He knew what he was doing and I ah . . . ah . . . I pretended he was you. That was the best part."

Jhonny stared at him.

"Gimme a chance, okay, Jhonny? I've been dying to ask you out, but you're the boss' son and everything . . ."

"I'll give you a chance . . . if you lay off letting the customers blow you."

Mike gave him the slow, lazy smile that always sent a flicker of heat right to Jhonny's cock.

"Deal. Say . . . I wanna go home and sleep this off. I got an early audition tomorrow. You wanna hang out after that?"

"Yes, I do."

Mike grinned. "I got your number off the work schedule. I'll call you. Been meaning to for weeks now . . ."

"You sure you're okay?"

"Yeah. I'm just beat. That fight in the bowling lane was freaky, man."

Jhonny nodded. In the midst of all the mayhem, this conversation was the nicest thing that had happened to him in weeks. He had no idea what he was supposed to be doing tomorrow, but he'd find time to see Mike.

Mike gave him a quick kiss of the cheek and limped off into the darkness. Jhonny found himself grinning, then remembered what a frickin' catastrophe the rest of the night had been. He checked his cell phone. His dad was nowhere to be found. Jhonny had been forced to give free passes to people for future games. Ever had helped clear out the alley. God . . . he never wanted to see another bowling ball as long as he lived.

Chris let out a long sigh from his perch on the window box. Ever limped over to him.

"Are you okay?" Jhonny asked.

"Yeah . . . I'm okay. Listen, we can't just leave him here," Ever said.

"Why not? His freak flag has been blowin' sky high tonight."

"I know. Let's just get him in the car and take him home."

"No. I really don't wanna." Jhonny felt petulant, but it couldn't be helped. Chris had never shown interest in Mike before, but all night he'd acted like the guy was some kind of Second Coming.

The sound of a car horn startled him. He stared at the brand new, black Camaro that pulled up beside him.

"Hey . . ." He remembered to say *Vanessa*, just in time. His sister beamed at him from the driver's seat.

"Need a ride?"

"No. I got my wheels, and the rain's stopped—"

"Oh, but Ever called me and said somebody stole 'em all."

"What?" Jhonny flipped out.

"Oops." Her gaze shifted back and forth between Jhonny and Ever.

"I meant to tell you," Ever said, "but it's been pretty crazy around here."

Yeah, it had. Jhonny walked over to his car and was dismayed to see it propped up on bricks. Whoever took his tires had come prepared.

"I can't believe they had time to remove all the frickin' tires."

Ever put a hand on his shoulder. "Sorry, man."

Jhonny kicked a brick. "I hate my fucking car." He flipped open his cell phone and called his insurance company. Their twenty-four-hour hotline number placed him on hold. He'd had so many calamites in the past twelve months he'd even used up all his AAA calls for the year. *Damn it.*

"Leave the car there," the emergency dispatcher told him. "I'll file a report. A claims adjuster will be in touch tomorrow."

With any luck, somebody would steal the damned car overnight. He smiled at the thought. A new car. A new man . . . and back home, a new spaceship. Maybe things were looking up after all.

He wandered back to his sister's car. The rain started again. He felt a little better about giving Chris a ride since Vanessa and Ever seemed determined not to leave the guy all alone in the parking lot, especially in this fresh downpour. Something was off though. He seemed lost . . . and so helpless.

"I want to go home," Chris said.

"Sure. No problem," Ever said.

"Do you have a motorcycle?" Chris asked.

"No."

"Shame." Chris looked lost again.

"Where do you live?" Ever asked.

Chris looked incredulous. "The valley of the kings, of course."

Was that code for some place not gay? What was with this guy, anyway?

"Valley of the kings?" Vanessa scrunched up her nose.

"But I don't want to go there. I want to go home with you, Ever. I like you." His loopy smile must have tugged at Ever's heart. Whatever the heck was going on with Chris, he was a lot nicer tonight than usual and, damn . . . the rain had kinda curled the ends of his hair, making him look hotter than ever.

Jhonny could tell Ever was stone-cold attracted to the guy. At least one of them would get to break his record-holding drought tonight.

"Okay," Ever said, glancing over at Jhonny, who gave him an encouraging nod. "Sure."

They all squeezed into Vanessa's car. "I want a word with you," she said to Ever, who sat beside her in the front seat. She cranked up the heat, which was noisy in her car. Jhonny leaned forward to listen better. It was hard with Chris crapping on about streetlights and the rain, and . . . now he was playing with his seat belt like it was a new toy.

"Vroom, vroom!" he chortled.

"I want to invest in your new business," Vanessa said over his childish cries.

Jhonny's mouth dropped open. He'd mentioned it to his mom. Vanessa must have been listening.

"Look," she said. "I work like a dog, and I've saved my bucks. I allow myself one indulgence. I buy a vintage *Barbie* doll a month on eBay. I love collecting, but what you and Jhonny do is impressive, and I'm interested. Besides, my last boyfriend hated all the dolls staring at him. He said it was like waking up to a bunch of *Stepford Wives*. I'm thinking . . . I've got some genuine collectible dolls, some real gems. Hey, I have a genuine Colleen Moore — remember the silent screen actress? — fairy dollhouse. Only ten were ever made, and I own one. I also have a genuine first edition Barbie from 1959, never played with, mint in box condition."

"That must be killing you," Ever said. "Aren't you dying to take her out of the box?"

"You have no idea. I itch to touch her. My point is this. I have some incredible things. Maybe we can even put them in your museum."

"The Colleen Moore dollhouse sounds amazing," Ever said. "I never even knew she made them. And you'd really let us show them?"

"I'd really let you show them."

Ever turned and looked over his shoulder at Jhonny. The two friends exchanged grins. Ever must have realized he had Jhonny's go-ahead.

"Well, come on in," he said to her, "and let's talk about this over coffee."

"Can I stay over?" she said. "I've got jammies and stuff in the trunk."

"Sure," Ever said.

Jhonny rolled his eyes. His sister spent more time bunking on the rollaway in their living room than she did at her own home. Still, if she was about to release her iron grip on her purse strings, he could put up with her for the night. He realized in that same moment how much these evenings meant to his sister. Loneliness, he decided, was a motherfucker.

The rain tapered off as they hurried from the car and trooped up the stairs to the triplex. Chris took in the apartment, a wide-eyed expression on his face. Ever took a moment of satisfaction to absorb the newcomer's appreciation of his home. Everyone had the same reaction.

"Visitors," Chris said, pointing to the *Lost in Space* ship still taking up a big chunk of the living room.

"You oughta see the costumes they have from *Lost in Space*. All the moon-walking outfits the Robinson family wore. A couple of robot prototypes, too. Wait 'til you see this place." Vanessa's eyes sparkled. She loved it but sometimes made fun of the apartment's contents.

"Can I show him around?" Her gaze went from Jhonny to Ever.

Ever nodded. She was welcome to it. He went to the kitchen and boiled water to make coffee as Jhonny leaned against one of the cabinets.

"So, you and Chris, huh?"

Ever shrugged. "We'll see what happens. He seems kinda . . . I don't know, sweet tonight. Don'tcha think?"

"Yeah. I'm just waiting for his inner rattlesnake to come out and bite us in the butt."

Ever shook his head. "I know what you mean, but I live in hope this sweet side is for real. We got any struffoli left?" Ever asked. His aunt had sent him a gigantic tin of the delicious Italian pastry puffs from Mona Lisa Bakery in New York. He and Jhonny had motor-boated through quite a few, and there was still half a tin left.

"They're still soft and fresh." Jhonny picked one out of the tin and bit into it.

"You have a visitor's suit," Chris said, poking his head into the door. "Where is the visitor?"

What was with the visitor crap?

"When did the *Jupiter II* land?" he asked.

Ever and Jhonny stared at each other.

"He must be a real fan," Ever said.

"Where is the visitor?" Chris seemed agitated.

"Do you mean Vanessa?" Jhonny asked.

"I must find him." Chris took off, and they followed him into the living room where Vanessa pointed out the sofa to Chris.

"That's from *I Love Lucy*," she said. "Remember the episode where she bought a new sofa and coffee table, and Ricky got mad?"

Chris just stared at her.

"Yeah, I know, Ricky got mad a lot. But this was the episode where she hid the new stuff in the kitchen and . . . and . . . she made dinner in the living room and put a little table in there and had to keep running through the Mertz's place to get stuff she'd forgotten."

"Lucy," he said, and patted the sofa cushion. He sat, his gaze on Ever's face. The expression there sent sparks of sexual heat right to Ever's cock.

"He's so funny tonight," Jhonny said. "Sit with him, Lucy. I'll bring out the coffee and pastries."

Ever sat. As Vanessa prattled about the new business venture, Ever wondered if Chris was going to say something weird and break the sweet little spell. But he didn't. He ate the pastries when Jhonny brought them out, closing his eyes as he ate.

"Almonds." He closed his eyes. "Very nice, Ever."

It was as if the guy hadn't eaten for a hundred years, the way he savored the flavor and commented on the colors. He sure hadn't been like that during their Cuban food truck outing.

He went crazy over the coffee. "I can taste its robustness," he said. "May I have more?"

Ever was happy to make more. Chris kept smiling and Ever made the obviously starving man a grilled cheese sandwich. This, too, got raves.

"What is this seed? Rye?"

Ever nodded. Wow, the guy was really out there tonight, but at least he'd knocked off the *visitor* crap. Vanessa helped him demolish a couple of sandwiches, a lot of pastries and a few cups of coffee on her own. And she never stopped talking. Ever didn't mind. They all let her talk. Chris seemed obsessed with CNN and laughed maniacally at a news story about the development of a new jet. He massaged Ever's shoulders with one hand, wielding the remote with the other. Ever was getting hornier by the second but tried to shake it off.

He glanced over at Jhonny, who fielded texts with Mike.

"I got a date with him for tomorrow." Jhonny looked ecstatic.

Ever was pleased to see his friend so happy. He felt pretty goddamned happy himself, experiencing a growing awareness emerging between him and Chris.

Chris's hand moved to Ever's lower back. He pressed a couple of points with his thumbs that appeared to go straight to Ever's groin. Sensations of lust and euphoria overtook him.

Just as quickly, Chris released his grip but inched even closer to him on the sofa, his body aligned with Ever's.

Thigh to thigh, hip to hip . . . God this guy was hot, and he longed to be alone with him.

"Can we watch a movie?" Vanessa suddenly asked. "You do have the best collection. She scooted on her knees over to the cabinet housing their DVDs. Ever's spirits dropped. He loved Vanessa and ordinarily would have loved having a movie and pajama party with her, but right now, he longed to be alone with Chris.

"I want to go to bed, Lucy," Chris announced.

Vanessa had a handful of DVDs in her hands and glanced up.

"Go," Jhonny insisted. "We'll stay up."

"Okay then." Ever winked at them both. "See you in the morning."

Alone at last, Ever hardly had time to close the door on the others before Chris took his hand, held it to his lips and asked, "May I?"

Ever nodded, startled. No man had ever kissed his hand this way, in such a gallant, reverent fashion. Chris held Ever's hand, grazing his knuckles with his lips, before turning his wrist and kissing the palm.

"Thank you," Chris muttered, his voice raspy and deep. "May I disrobe you?"

Disrobe me? In spite of his funny language and unusual behavior, Ever was enthralled. The guy wanted him, and he wanted Chris.

Chris stepped forward, removing Ever's clothing piece by piece, his gaze feverish looking.

"It's been so long for me." His voice, a low moan, seemed to caress Ever's body the same way his hands were. Chris brushed his fingertips along Ever's arms and throat, down his torso, the back of his hands rubbing lightly against Ever's nipples. The knuckles kept moving back and forth, their slight roughness igniting a thrill in Ever that shot straight to his cock. Dang. This guy had some magic hands on him.

"How long?" Ever asked, trying to keep his breathing steady.

Chris looked into his eyes. "Hundreds and hundreds of years."

Ever smiled. Chris was so endearing. Somehow, it made him feel better to think it had been a while since the guy had gotten laid. It would have taken the wind out of his romantic sails if Chris had said, *two days.*

Chris bent his head and kissed him. Ever was surprised how deep and erotic the embrace was. Chris seemed intent on tasting him, shocking him by licking and sucking his tongue. Ever began to worry about his possibly stinky breath, but Chris kept up his exploration of Ever's mouth in a languid way. Ever felt woozy until Chris's tongue shot to the roof of his mouth, touching a spot that sent fissures of fire through his body and fractions of dazzling color and light into his brain. Ever gasped.

What the hell is happening to me?

Chris gave him a hint of a smile as he moved down to Ever's nipples and sucked. And sucked. He took his time, Ever feeling like he was melting. Chris was nowhere near his cock but Ever was ready to explode. He longed for Chris's hand on his cock. He yearned for the other man's touch as he soared to a swift release. But it was not to be.

"Wait," Chris urged. "Just a little longer. You won't regret it."

Ever wasn't so sure. His cock bounced in front of him.

Chris glanced down at him, his smile wide now. "Sacred beauty," he whispered. His thumb slid along the length of the shaft. One more slide and Ever would have come all over the man's hand. Instead, Chris placed a kiss on Ever's shoulder and told him to lie on the bed.

Ever did as he was told, watching Chris, er . . . disrobe. The man had a hot body that made his cock leap again. *Oh boy. Oh boy, oh boy, oh boy! He's got a nice big juicy cock for me to play with.*

"On your knees," Chris said.

Ever turned around, raising himself up as Chris got behind him and began licking and kissing his back. Chris's tongue dipped into his hips and down his ass crack, Ever's whole body poised in anticipation as that hot tongue made a beeline for his asshole.

"Arrggh!" Ever felt the orgasm starting in his tailbone. There was no holding it, but Chris didn't seem to want him to wait any longer. He kept his tongue inside Ever, one hand slipping between his legs and grabbing Chris's cock. The slight contact was all it took. Ever came hard, his whole body vibrating with the force of his pent-up release. Chris hadn't asked, but it had been months for him. He saw stars and a couple of million galaxies in a purple and milky white way inside his head.

Chris Coelho was one heck of a magic carpet ride.

He kept up his stroking and touching and that blessed, infernal ass-licking.

Ever's cock remained rigid. He found himself breathing hard again, backing up, humping Chris's face.

"On your back," Chris said. For the first time, his mouth came down to take possession of Ever's cock. His ass rose from the bed as Chris swallowed his cock in small increments, making growling, mewling sounds in the rear of his throat that sent pleasurable sensations to Ever's ever-ready shaft.

"I want you to come with my life-force in you," Chris said, his voice reaching Ever from a thick, but pleasurable sex fog.

"Yeah, yeah, fuck me," he begged, opening up his legs. He was going to come again. He adored getting fucked but put his hands on Chris's chest as the man knelt, poised between his spread thighs.

"Hon, you gotta put on a rubber," he said.

Ever pointed to the wooden box on his bedside table, reaching across to open it. He withdrew a few foils of Kimono condoms, his favorite. He loved their sheer texture and almost sweet smell. He handed one to Chris, who stared at it.

"Gotta take a leak," Ever said, running to his private bathroom. He peed, door ajar, staring at his cheeks. His face had the 'just fucked' flush he hadn't seen there for a long, long time. And the man hadn't even been inside him yet. The thought of having that beautiful prick inside him made him smile.

He washed his hands and ran back to the bed only to find Chris struggling to get the condom on his left foot.

"What the fuck?" He stared at Chris, who glanced up at him as the Kimono broke.

"Dude, I hope this is a joke. You don't think you're going to shove your foot into my ass do you?"

"No." Chris looked bewildered. "Why would I think that?"

"You're such a clown."

Ever bent and kissed him, then got on the bed and began sucking Chris's cock. He was a receptive, joyous lover who responded as enthusiastically as Ever had. Ever could no longer wait. He ripped open another square foil and rolled the velvety rubber over Chris's cock with his mouth.

"Oooh . . ." Chris watched him, his eyes huge.

"Now," Ever said, "let me have that cock."

Chris scooted between his legs, his raging cock tangling with Ever's. He stroked them both with one hand, staring down into Ever's eyes, allowing his cock to move down Ever's groin. Ever loved how Chris made every single gesture so erotic and intimate. He begged Chris to fuck him. The lube on the Kimono was just right. Chris's cock was slick and deliciously hard as he began working once again on Ever's hole. He entered Ever slowly, both of them crying out as Ever adjusted to his size.

God help me. He's huge!

"How sweet you are," Chris murmured when he was finally fully immersed. He fucked Ever relentlessly until they came together, a rare occurrence for Ever, who grinned and laughed as Chris's whole face changed, his pleasure bringing out a childlike expression to his countenance.

Chris's head dropped onto Ever's shoulder. Ever lay underneath him, his spent cock still leaking against Chris's belly and his own.

"More?" Chris asked.

"Yeah, yeah." Ever couldn't say anything else. Especially when Chris turned him over once again and began sucking and licking his ass.

"Fuck!" Ever shouted. "You are so hot!"

Jhonny heard the pounding on the front door and sat up on the sofa. Disoriented for a moment, he remembered he'd fallen asleep watching a movie. He'd been doing that a lot lately. His back hurt as he swung his feet to floor. He stumbled to the door and opened it.

His mad old landlady stood on her toes, screaming at him as soon as she saw his face.

"There's a naked man in the front yard," she shouted.

"Why are you telling me? Call the police."

"He's a friend of yours." She dropped her voice. "This is a respectable neighborhood and a very reputable triplex. We don't do naked men on the front lawn here."

"And you say he's a friend of mine?"

"I saw him walking out of here fifteen minutes ago.

Scratching his nuts, you know."

"No, I don't know." Jhonny looked beyond her bony shoulders and gaped. Chris Coelho was out front on his knees, naked, just as she said, except his arms were raised to the sky, and he was screaming some strange . . . incantation.

What the fuck?

"Sorry, Mrs. Zapel, leave it to me."

She grunted. In her youth, she claimed she'd been a female boxer, and sometimes Jhonny believed it. She had a fighter's stance and a mean personality to match. She could turn the charm on and off, but it had no dimmer switch. She either adored you or hated you.

"Make it snappy, kid. I don't want my property values falling."

Yeah, right. According to her, empty bottles in the trash reduced property values.

"Sorry, Mrs. Zapel. Right away, Mrs. Zapel." He was sorry now that he had allowed Ever to talk him into bringing Chris back here. Why couldn't he have stayed in Ever's room bumping uglies with him?

He waited until she'd returned next door before knocking on Ever's door until his roommate called out.

"I'm awake!"

Jhonny opened the door and poked his head around it.

"Your boyfriend's out front doing a rain dance."

"Say, what?"

"Naked. The old the cat's been 'round here frothing at the mouth."

"Are you sure? He was here a few minutes ago."

"I'm sure. He's out there making an ass of himself."

"Oh, God." Ever reached to the floor for his jeans, sliding them up his legs. "I gotta take a leak. Be right there."

Jhonny gave him a little privacy, waiting in the living room. He peered out the window. Chris was now bowing down low, raising his arms up . . . What was he doing?

Praying?

He wasn't speaking English, and people had started to gather out front.

Ever joined him, looking outside.

"Oh, God." He rushed back to his room, returning with a blanket. "The things you see when you don't have a tranquilizer gun."

He ran out front, Jhonny watching in some amusement as Ever struggled to get the blanket around the guy, who resisted him. Jhonny went outside to help him, surprised at how strong Chris was.

"You so owe me," Jhonny hissed as Chris's flailing arms hit him in the face.

"I don't understand it. He was so frickin' hot last night, and now he's acting like a goddam headcase. Chris. Stop it!"

They got him back inside. Chris allowed them to put him on the sofa.

Vanessa came out of Jhonny's bathroom, where she'd been showering and changing.

"Holy moly," she said, reaching for her makeup bag. "Is he naked?"

Jhonny nodded.

Vanessa grinned. *He's huge,* she mouthed retreating to the bathroom.

"I don't get it, Chris. What the hell happened to you?" Ever asked, kneeling in front of the guy.

Chris looked at him, a weird expression on his face.

"Morning prayer," he said. "I have you. I have so much to be grateful for

CHAPTER FOUR

"Don't look at me like that, Jhonny," Ever said. "Say something."

"I don't even know *what* to say except . . . Ya know, I've heard about crazy chick sex, but crazy guy sex is a new one on me."

"Thanks a bunch." Ever shook his head.

"Seriously. Dude. Crazy girl sex usually involves appendages being stapled and unpleasant objects shoved up asses . . . but um . . . condoms on your feet is pretty up there in the weirdness category."

"Thanks again."

"C'mon, you know it's weird."

"Of course I do. I just . . . I thought it was a joke."

"A joke?"

"You had to be there."

"Noooo . . . .hearing about it is painful enough."

"Jhonny, I swear . . . it was like he had no idea what to do with a frickin' rubber!"

Ever put his ear to the closed bathroom door.

"Any sign of life?" Jhonny glanced at his roommate's worried expression. Ever had convinced Chris to come inside and now the guy was locked in the bathroom. Jhonny's bathroom. He was alone and suspiciously quiet. It had been that way for forty-five minutes.

"Maybe he's praying again," Jhonny said.

The frustrated expression on Ever's face was priceless. "Chris?" He tapped lightly on the door. "You okay in there?"

"Uh-huh." Chris threw open the door, stark naked.

"Why the hell aren't you dressed?" Jhonny couldn't help venting some steam. He and Ever had an appointment at nine and Chris had been in there for freaking *ever*.

"Dressed? Oh." Chris looked befuddled as he brushed past them into Ever's bedroom.

Jhonny nudged his roommate. "Maybe you should go in there and egg him on. Dude. We are so late. It's after eight-thirty."

Ever sighed. "I don't wanna go in there. Two seconds alone with him and I wanna get naked and do the funky chicken with him."

"Damn. He's that good, huh?" Jhonny had to admit, the guy had a huge dick, and he walked with a pretty confident swagger. He just couldn't forget that Chris Coelho was also a frickin' tool.

"Yeah, he is that good, as a matter of fact. Except for the thing with condoms, and the naked praying, he's damned hot."

He walked off to his room. Jhonny heard him coaxing Chris into getting changed.

"Get your hands off me," he heard Ever saying. He heard kissing, a zipper being lowered and, God help him, the sounds of sucking.

"We gotta go!" Jhonny yelled out.

Thirty seconds later, Ever was coming out of the bedroom, Chris behind him. He was dressed except for his socks and shoes.

"Are we ready?" Jhonny worked hard to keep his temper under control.

"We're ready." Ever seemed strained. As Chris sat on the sofa, rolling his socks on his feet and putting his shoes on, Ever grabbed Jhonny and dragged him into the hall.

"He won't tell me where he needs to go."

"What do you mean?"

Ever spread his hands. "He has no idea where he parked his car yesterday. I'm guessing it's back at the museum."

Vanessa chose that moment to emerge from the bathroom wearing so much makeup Jhonny almost gagged.

"What's the matter?" she asked, throwing all her stuff into two bags that spent their entire lives in her trunk. Vanessa adored living out of them. She carried numerous changes of clothing and slept at various friends' places overnight just to get away from her own loneliness. She had a nice condo in Encino but never wanted to be there.

"We think Chris left his car at the museum yesterday," Jhonny said. "He's not saying."

Chris was now bent over his shoes, studying them.

"Aww . . . I think it's sweet," Vanessa said. "He doesn't want to leave Ever. Tell you what, I'll drop him wherever he needs to go. You get outta here. I know you've gotta meet Mac."

"We owe you," Ever said.

"Yeah, you do." She offered her cheeks for kisses.

"Vanessa's going to drop you at work," Ever told Chris.

"Can't I have a kiss, too?" Chris got to his feet, towering over Ever, who offered his tilted face up for a kiss. It turned hot quickly.

"Jesus, you two. Could ya hit the dimmer switch?" Jhonny yanked at Ever, who looked moon-faced at Chris. "Come on, guy, we gotta book."

Ever gave Chris a finger wave. Chris seemed bereft.

"I'll look after him." Vanessa threaded her arm through Chris's, waving them away.

Outside, Ever dropped his keys twice before he could unlock his car door.

"You're a mess," Jhonny observed.

"Tell me about it. I've had more sex in the last nine hours than I've had in a whole year."

"Well, that's good, right? I'm hoping I break my record soon, as well."

Ever fired up his old BMW, gripping the steering wheel.

"Man, I forgot how good it feels to fuck. Jhonny, we can't let it wait so long between . . . you know, rides around the park. We gotta get back on our bikes more often."

"Vroom, vroom." Jhonny felt bad imitating Chris, but it had been weird. All of it, seriously weird. "He kept asking if I had a motorcycle." His heart softened for a moment. Chris had turned out to be a big kid. They'd never seen this side of him before. Suddenly, it irked him that Ever never had problems with his fourteen-year-old car. But how could he begrudge him that? Ever was a good guy. The best guy. Why couldn't they have fallen in love with each other?

"You worried about your car?" Ever asked, reading him accurately as always.

"Yeah." Jhonny tried not to worry about how much of his own car was still left in the bowling alley parking lot. "We can't do anything until the insurance adjuster can meet us there."

"No problem. I'll take you wherever you need to go today."

"Cool, thanks. Nothing pressing. Say . . . what was the Egyptian exhibit like?"

"Amazing. There were mummies from all over the world. It was really cool."

Jhonny let Ever tell him all about it as they drove along Magnolia, hooking a right on Laurel Canyon. They headed north to Chandler, moving slowly in the heavy early-morning traffic.

Mac McCready was already waiting for them in the parking lot on the northwest corner of Laurel Canyon. Dressed like a cowboy, their scarily thin, seventy-three-year-old buddy waved from outside the empty lot. Ever drove in, parking just inside the entrance. They got out of the car and sauntered over to Mac, who once worked as a cowboy on Universal Studios' westerns, or *oaters*, as they were known in industry circles.

He'd traveled the world with Clint Eastwood and other major stars, taking the falls off horses and saloon rooftops for them until crippling injuries sidelined his stuntman career. He now choreographed Universal Studios' western show, which performed daily for the tour right on the lot. He did this for a living and scavenged the city for Tinseltown memorabilia for his major, life-absorbing hobby.

Jhonny scanned the lot, wondering what memorabilia there was to be found here.

Mac's spidery hand shot out, and they took turns shaking it. He was so thin and veiny, Jhonny always worried the guy's arm would rip right out of its socket.

"What gives?" Ever asked. "What have you found?"

"That." He jabbed an index finger up in the air, and the two roommates glanced up. Sure enough, in the corner of the otherwise barren space stood a blue sign saying Gibraltar Savings.

"Oh, man." Ever groaned. Jhonny seconded the emotion. The last time they'd done a bank job for Mac it had ended up costing them a lot of money.

"You want the sign?" Jhonny asked.

"Yeah. They've been out of business twenty-nine years, and I checked it out. The property owner's only too happy for me to take it off his hands."

The two roommates exchanged looks. That's what Mac always said. He had a peculiar fondness for old bank signs. He had easily a hundred of them that once belonged to defunct institutions. His reasoning, he claimed, was that he liked the reminder that he'd outlived *the big guns.*

"I'll give you five grand. I even have a beautiful place to put it." He handed them a photograph. Jhonny grinned. It was the garden of Mac's ramshackle but now valuable Mulholland Drive property. He'd bought it for thirteen thousand dollars in the fifties, and it was now worth over three million smackers. He lived on a narrow artery off the main highway in a thicket of dense vegetation. The sound of coyotes hunting and demolishing prey was his night music. He wanted the sign to join his unusual collection, including Lytton Savings and Loan, Farmers and Merchant and Vineyard Bank.

Lytton Savings and Loan had been a special revenge for Mac. It had been built on the site of what had once been the amazing and fabled Garden of Allah. The lush gardens and majestic, twenty-five villa extravaganzas sprawling through the middle of it had been the creation of notorious silent screen actress, Alla Nazimova, in 1927. It later became a Hollywood landmark hotel famed for its decadent parties immortalized in movies and novels. F. Scott Fitzgerald had lived there during his screenwriting days, having a wild affair there with writer Sheilah Graham while his wife Zelda languished in a sanitarium.

Nazimova sold the property but kept one villa for her own use, the others used as rental apartments for an astonishing array of international celebrities for four decades. The Garden of Allah's importance in Hollywood history be damned. In 1959, the mythical, lauded property was demolished for the bank and a gigantic parking lot on the corner of Sunset and Crescent Heights. A replica of the original building and its exquisite gardens was made and kept on display outside Lytton Savings and Loan under a huge Perspex bubble until 2007 when it was moved into the lobby. When Lytton Savings and Loan went under, the display mysteriously disappeared.

It wasn't much of a mystery to Jhonny and Ever since the display was now in their proud possession. It would be a real signature piece for their museum. It had cost them a bundle to buy the display from friends of Mac's. The old Lytton Savings and Loan sign now stood in his backyard, and he liked to tell people his dogs enjoyed peeing on it. If he had a say in it, they would also get to lift their legs on what was left of Gibraltar Savings.

Jhonny found himself humming the lyrics of 'Big Yellow Taxi,' the song Joni Mitchell penned in 1970 about the fall of the Garden of Allah. She had been so right. They'd demolished paradise and put up a parking lot. They'd done the same thing here, too. All over Los Angeles, history had given way for designated, off-street parking.

Ever grinned. "I was just thinking about the Garden of Allah."

"Aw ... you guys are making me feel real sentimental." Mac had been a long-term resident of the hotel and its subsequent transformation into luxury apartments. Jhonny and Ever loved poring through his photo albums of his years there.

The two roommates traded glances. Five thousand dollars was a lot of money, and Mac had never failed to pay them for their work, and not just financially. He always tipped them off to hot Hollywood finds.

"So what's this I hear about you opening a tour and a museum?" Mac spat an ugly wad of brown goo beside Jhonny's foot, pawing through his tin of Red Man for a fresh pat of chewing tobacco. "And when were you gonna invite me to join in the fun?"

His big, toothy grin, the promise of five K and the irresistible offer of financial investment meant a big yes to the big bank sign.

It would cost them close to Mac's price to get the sign

down and hauled to his house, but it would be worth it.

"Let's go grab a coffee at Twain's and talk," Mac said. "I want the sign by Friday. Think you fellas can manage that?"

Ever and Jhonny nodded. It would be rough getting that thing down. They studied the pole embedded in the ground. Rough, tough and just how Mac liked it.

"I must have driven past this intersection a million times and never noticed this sign," Jhonny said, photographing the bolts securing the sign to the pavement.

"Yeah, well, it's all for a good cause." Mac rocked on his heels, staring up at the sign. One man's defunct bank was another man's Garden of Allah.

They followed Mac down to Twain's, one of the last re-maining diners in LA. Stunned to find it shuttered and awaiting demolition, then they motored over to Jerry's Deli.

"Our history's disappearing," Ever muttered. Out of no-where, a motorcycle roared. He jumped. "What was that?"

"What was what?" Mac asked.

"Aw, it's nothing." *I'm just losing my mind, that's all.* Ever slumped into silence as Mac and Jhonny debated where to nosh.

Fifteen minutes later over bagels and coffee, they ran the museum plan down for Mac, who seemed excited. The check came just as Jhonny's insurance adjuster called saying he was on his way to Gallo Lanes. Mac took the opportunity to gross out the waitress and his breakfast companions by tak-ing his teeth out of his mouth.

"I got the check," he said, inspecting his dentures for crumbs.

Ever tried not to react. He wasn't sure which was worse — Mac removing his teeth or his hair. The two roommates thanked him and excused themselves and headed over to the bowling alley.

Workers stood outside the bowling alley, stowing away tools in their truck.

"Oh, hey." Ever recognized the technician who'd helped him the night before. "You were great last night, thanks. By the way, I don't know your name."

The technician shook his hand, grinning. "Darren Stevens."

Ever thought he was hearing things. "As in the guy married to Samantha on *Bewitched*?"

"Yeah." The guy chuckled. "Except mine is spelled Darren with an e, not an I. At least people like him. I'm glad my dumb-ass mom didn't call me Attila or something."

Ever laughed. Wait until Jhonny found out the guy's name.

"The lanes are all fixed and good to go," Darren said, "except the place smells like barf."

Ever grinned. Good old Waldo. His cleaning was up to its usual substandard quality.

"Bummer. Bum fucking bummer!" Jhonny shouted at him across the parking lot.

Ever sauntered over.

"Can you believe it? My car is still here. Why don't they just steal it and be done with it already?"

"Why don't you just sell it?"

"I will *not* sell a haunted car to some other poor, unsuspecting schmo." Jhonny's tone was indignant.

"Too bad it's not vintage enough to qualify for our museum." Ever paused. "You know . . . that's not a bad idea."

"What?" Jhonny stared at him.

"Pitching it as a haunted car. This is LA. Some wacko will think that's a pretty good deal."

"Yeah." Jhonny looked depressed. He blew out an aggrieved sigh. "I have a confession."

Ever arched a brow in his direction.

"The original seller tried to tell me it was haunted. I thought he was off his rocker."

Ever laughed. "Are you kidding me?"

Jhonny grinned. When you looked at it, it was pretty damned funny.

While they waited for the insurance adjuster, they went inside the bowling alley. A few bowlers were making use of the almost empty building. Jhonny's dad, Jimmy Gallo, sat slumped at his desk, a half-finished Sudoku puzzle at his elbow.

"I went around the corner for a few limoncellos last night and came back to find the place in total disarray," he grumped.

"A few limoncellos? Dad, you were gone for *hours*."

"What the hell happened here last night?" Jimmy fumed

They tried to explain, but it seemed he didn't want to hear.

"And why does it stink of barf?" he whined, interrupting Ever's detailed description of Franklin Rambo's assault.

After giving them a hard time for a few more minutes, he'd vented enough of his spleen to focus on his next point of rage, his missing security guard.

"What's up with that Chris Coelho character anyway? He never showed up this morning."

"He was supposed to be here?" Ever was surprised. As far as he knew, Vanessa had taken him to the museum. Oh well, Chris was a big boy, he could fend for himself.

"I called Mike Fletcher, and he's gonna come in early and cover for him," Jimmy said. "He's got an audition on some soap opera, and then he's coming right over." He leaned across the desk and lowered his voice. "Between you, me, and the bowling balls, guy has about as much talent as my hangnail."

"That never stopped anybody from getting a movie career," Ever said. He felt bad for Jhonny, who was supposed to be meeting Mike for lunch.

"Yeah, I guess that's true, but he's a good security guard. Gets along with everybody." Jimmy frowned suddenly. "Middle-aged men really seem to like him. They all want to bowl on his shifts."

Oh, boy.

Jhonny opened his mouth but Ever dragged him away before he could say something he'd regret.

"Did you hear that? Huh? Huh? He was trying to tell me last night that what happened in the john was a one-off. Christ. What am I, a deadbeat magnet?"

"No. Now let's not overreact. You're not in a relationship with him yet. Let's give him a chance."

"You think?"

Ever nodded. "I think."

Jhonny grinned at him. "You're always good for talking me down off ledges, bro."

"Backatcha."

"You think Mike might get that soap opera?"

"Who knows? He's a good-looking guy. He's got the right look for soap."

Jhonny eyed him. "He does, doesn't he? Kinda . . . straight, all-American looking."

"Yeah."

For some reason, the idea of a budding soap opera star in the ultra-conservative world of daytime TV getting head from middle-aged men in a bowling alley restroom made Ever smile. He caught Jhonny's glance, and they busted up. Without fail, they could always reach other's minds.

"Oh . . . man," Jhonny said, at last, wiping his eyes. "I needed that laugh."

They walked outside and found the insurance guy circling Jhonny's vehicle. Well, what *used* to be the vehicle. All that was left of it were the four stacks of bricks that had propped it up the day before.

"Holy shit, don't tell me it got stolen?" Jhonny couldn't hide his glee.

"No." The adjuster looked sheepish. "I just had it towed. I'm sorry to tell you I accidentally rear-ended you. I think we can safely say it's a total write-off. Here's my report. Sorry about that. I'll make sure you get well compensated."

Jhonny's smile was so wide, he could barely speak. "A total write-off, you say?"

"Yeah. Man. It was the freakiest thing. I saw this naked guy walking around, and I took my eyes off the lot for a moment, and he jumped right out at me. I swerved to avoid him and smacked right into your car."

Naked man. Ever and Jhonny exchanged looks. Was Chris here someplace, running around in the nude?

"It was freaky. He asked me if I knew where P. Diddy's temple was . . . or at least I think that's what he said. He told me he was looking for the valley of the kings. Anyway . . . I gotta book, guys. Have a nice day!"

Oh, it was Chris for sure.

"Any idea where he went?" Jhonny called out as the guy walked away.

The adjuster turned, scratching his chin. "Yeah. I saw him walking up Whitsett."

Jhonny and Ever jumped back into Ever's car. As he drove, Jhonny called Vanessa from his cell phone.

"He kept saying he wanted to go home . . . something about P. Diddy. Christ, he's a scary mofo," she said. "He started to cry. Since he was wearing his security guard uniform, I dropped him at the bowling alley because he got really upset when I tried to take him to the museum."

"Wait . . . he started to cry?"

"Yeah. That's a guy who takes his work seriously, ya

know? I figured he was late for his bowling alley shift."

"There he is," Ever shouted suddenly.

"We found him, sis." Jhonny ended the call. They spotted Chris waiting at the lights. He wasn't quite naked. He still wore boxer briefs, socks, and shoes.

"Hey there." His face lit up when Ever stopped beside them.

"Where are your clothes?" Jhonny asked, climbing out of the car.

Chris put a finger to his chin. He seemed to be thinking about it. "Um . . . I forget."

"Get in."

A bus honked them, so Jhonny shoved the guy into the front seat, unlocked the back door and climbed into the back seat. Ever drove away as the bus driver honked him yet again.

"What's the matter with you?" Ever asked Chris. "Where are your goddamn clothes?"

"I gave them away. I saw this man . . ." He waved his hand around. "Ever . . . it's so good to see you again. I missed you. Or do you prefer Lucy?"

"What?" Ever stared at him, narrowly avoiding rear-ending the vehicle in front of him.

The expression on Chris's face was so lovelorn and goopy Ever melted for one brief second. *He missed me? This is a little . . . nutso. I just saw him a couple of hours ago.*

His temper flared. "I'm Ever. Not Lucy. Goddamn it, Chris, you're acting like a real wacko. You need meds or something?"

"I am? Oh." Chris fell silent. Ever immediately felt guilty. The guy looked devastated.

"Let's get him home. Where does he live?" Jhonny asked from the backseat.

"I don't know. Chris, where do you live?"

"In the valley of the kings."

"Oh, man . . . not that again."

Chris nodded emphatically. "Oh, yes, in the temple of Pi Di Amen. We need to hurry. I am late for morning prayers."

Ever stomped on the brake, almost causing an accident with the enraged bus driver, who lay on the horn now. Ever turned the corner, getting off the main road. He idled at the red zone.

"Okay, Chris . . . enough with the valley of the kings crap. If it's some kind of code, it's lost on me. Where do you live?" He enunciated his words carefully. The guy was beginning to really creep him out.

"I told you, Ever. I live in the temple of Pi Di Amen."

"Where's your wallet? Your driver's license must have your address."

Chris put his finger to his chin again. "I don't know."

"Okay." Ever wondered if the guy had lasting repercussions from his head injury in the last twenty-four hours.

"Maybe we should get you to a doctor. I think you have concussion." He started to panic. What if he'd taken sexual advantage of a guy who was technically sleepwalking or in some kind of fugue state?

"I don't have a concussion," Chris said in a convincing tone. "The paramedics checked me out last night. My pulse and response rates are normal. That I do know. My head doesn't hurt. A physician knows these things."

Ever stared at him. "You're a physician? I didn't know that."

"Oh, yes. I know a lot, Ever. I just don't remember some . . . things."

Now he was sounding really cuckoo.

"Who did you give your clothes to?" Jhonny leaned over from the backseat, his tone soothing. Ever felt grateful he had his roommate with him.

"Oh . . . that was a poor man on the street. He said he

needed bread. I had no bread. I offered him my clothing." Chris frowned. "He didn't seem very appreciative."

Ever laughed. "No, I bet he didn't."

Chris suddenly pointed. "Look that's him now."

They all stared across the road. The man in question was asleep on a bus bench, newspaper covering him. Chris's clothes lay in a discarded heap on the ground by the trash barrel.

"I'll get them. Stay there," Ever said, marching across the road.

"Ever, I am hungry!" Chris shouted after him.

The drunk emanated a foul odor of cheap booze and cigarettes.

"Got any bread, man?" he asked, raising his head as Ever reached him. "Got any change?"

Ever fished into his pocket and handed him a buck.

"My friend left his clothes here. I'm just going to take them back."

"Whatever." The guy looked grumpy as he palmed the money with a grimy hand.

Ever walked back across the road and felt along the pockets. A wallet. *Bingo.*

He pulled it out and, as he climbed into the car, he threw Chris's clothing to him.

"I know they've been on the ground, but you gotta put 'em on. You can't drive around in your underwear. You'll get arrested for indecent exposure. Put 'em on for now, and we'll get you home, and you can change."

"But I don't wanna go home."

"You just said you did. Here's your wallet, pal. Can I check your ID?"

Chris just stared at him.

"Oh, for chrissakes." Ever flipped open the brown leather wallet and examined the license. Chris lived in Silverlake.

Christ. It wasn't far, but it was really out of the way and Ever and Jhonny had calls in to a couple of friends with two
trucks and removal vans. They needed to be ready to head
back over to remove the Gibraltar Savings sign.

Chris got out of the car to put on his clothes. As they sat
there waiting, a car horn honk jolted them out of their an-
guished reverie. Vanessa's car swerved in front of them. She
braked hard, left the engine running and came over to them.

"Hey, I'm so glad I found you. I felt kinda guilty dropping loopy chops here at the bowling alley, especially when
Dad said he hadn't been inside. I've been driving around
looking at him. Why's he half naked?"

"You don't want to know," Ever said.

Jhonny's cell phone rang. He took the call. "It's the owner
of the lot on Chandler. We can have the sign. Mac wasn't
BSing."

"Cool," Ever said. His cell phone rang. He didn't recognize the number.

"Hey," a man's voice said. "This is Darren Stevens, you
know, from the bowling alley?"

"Oh, hey. Of course."

"Listen, I just got a call from a friend. He said you need
something heavy lifted. I have a hydraulic truck. I can do it."

Ever repeated the news to Jhonny, who gave him a
thumbs up. Ever told him they'd need two guys.

"I'm here," Chris said, obviously listening to every word.
He was fully dressed and back in the passenger seat. "Lemme help. Please?"

Ever caved in. He was a big guy, and it beat having to get
him over to Silverlake.

"Okay," he said.

Vanessa gave them a wave and ran back to her car.

At the lot on Chandler, Chris sauntered over to the huge
sign. He inspected it as Darren turned into the empty lot in

his massive, gadget-laden truck.

"Hey," Chris called over to Ever. "Is this all you need? This post pulled from here?"

"Wait," Ever said. "We need bolt cutters and—"

Chris gripped the pole and heaved. With a strange, super-human cry, he roared, pulling the pole right out of the ground. It was if time stood still, the sound of metal and concrete ripping.

"Oh, my God," Darren muttered. "What the hell?"

He ran over. Ever, Jhonny, and Darren stared at Chris as he tore up half of Chandler Boulevard along with the bank sign.

"Where do you want it?" he asked, grinning at Ever.

CHAPTER FIVE

Mac was in orbit as they entered his private Shangri-La with his new sign. As long as he lived, Ever would never get tired of visiting Mac's mountain property. He had done little to improve on the old bungalow that he'd originally purchased, investing all his money in memorabilia. But oh, he had some treasures. Once they hauled the bank sign over to the spot Mac had selected, Darren and Chris worked on securing it into the foundations.

"I brought libations," Mac said, bringing out a tray loaded with bottles of Mike's Hard Lemonade. It was the perfect drink for hard work on a hot day.

Ever and Jhonny let Darren and Chris work on the installation of the sign, which now looked like it had always been here. Clinking bottles, they toasted each other. It was worth splitting the check Mac had given them four ways. The job was done, and Chris and Darren made the final part seem effortless.

"There," Darren said. "You know what, this is really a cool joint."

"Take a look around." Mac waved his hand airily, sliding onto a chaise longue in the middle of a thicket of bright green bamboo. "I wanna lay up here like a Muppet, admiring my sign. Ever and Jhonny can show you around. They've been here a million times."

Ever handed Darren and Chris chilled bottles. He tried not to think about the tug in his groin when Chris smiled at him. He let Jhonny lead the way through the various sections Mac had lovingly created. Ever tried not to think about having hot monkey sex up here in the middle of nowhere with Chris.

"Should we start with the tikis?" Jhonny asked.

"Sure." Ever grinned as Chris's hand landed on his butt. Chris gave it a squeeze and Ever's heart raced. Fuck. Chris got him all worked up without any apparent effort.

His new lover allowed Jhonny to distract him by leading them through an impressive collection of gigantic tikis that looked right at home in some lush, dense foliage.

"The ones on the right all came from Trader Vic's in Beverly Hills," Jhonny said. "It closed down a couple of years ago, and Mac bought up almost all of 'em. He even snapped up their drinks-for-two cocktail bowls."

"What about this?" Chris pointed to a set of darkly tropical tikis lacquered red.

"They came from Wan-Q, a Chinese-Hawaiian restaurant that used to be on Pico," Jhonny told him.

"I remember going there, and all the waiters wore Hawaiian shirts," Ever said. "This one waiter would run up and down the tables asking, 'Are you joosh?' It took me forever to figure out he was asking if we were Jewish since it was right near a Jewish temple and people stopped by for a quick meal before going to temple."

"Are you joosh?" Chris asked.

"No." Ever smiled. "What about you?"

"My people celebrate many gods," Chris responded, his expression grave.

Ever didn't know what to say. He just changed the subject as the four of them waded past a pristine collection of grass huts that once graced tiki bars up and down the Pacific coast.

"Say . . . this looks like it's a working bar," Darren asked, leaning over the grass-fringed counter that came from the defunct The Hut, a gigantic Polynesian restaurant.

"It is, in the summer." Ever pointed to all the bottles lined up on a shelf. "Mac likes to entertain. He has some wicked good parties. He's the host with the most."

They came across a booth from Alan Hale's Lobster Barrel, a one-time seafood joint the former captain of *Gilligan's Island* owned.

"I loved Gilligan!" Darren enthused.

"Me, too," Jhonny said. "My dad took me and my sister to Alan Hale's, and he seated us himself. He called me 'little buddy,' just like I was Gilligan." He paused, emotion crossing his face. "He was a lovely man. I'm lucky I got to meet him. My mom has a photo of me with Alan Hale that my dad took."

Darren stared. "I never knew he had a restaurant."

"Right on La Cienega," Ever said. "He had it for what? Fifteen years?"

"Yep." Jhonny nodded. "He ran it as long as he could, then in the late eighties he closed it down and opened a travel agency. Can you imagine booking a trip through the guy that got Gilligan and the others shipwrecked?"

The others laughed.

They walked through the old restaurant signs for Ships 24-hour diner, The Brown Derby (complete with the illustration of a brown derby hat), Tail o' the Cock (with a big chicken over the name), Chasen's, Sambo's Pancakes, and so many others.

"There used to be a Lone Ranger restaurant?" Darren asked.

"I think there were five. Hamburger joints. But we never went. They were before our time," Jhonny said. "Mac has funny stories about them though. He says Clayton Moore, who played *The Lone Ranger* on TV, owned them and he would greet the customers. If he liked you, he gave you a silver bullet."

"Yeah," Ever said. "He also said that the hamburgers were awful."

"Godawful." Jhonny grinned.

Ever felt Chris's hand on his butt again. It felt good but made the sexual heat flush right up his body, his neck and prickle at his hairline.

"He said the hamburgers were so tough it made you wonder what the hell ever happened to Silver," Ever said.

The others roared with laughter.

"Who's Silver?" Chris wanted to know.

"His horse."

"I thought maybe it was his motorcycle."

"What's with you and motorcycles?" Jhonny asked.

Chris frowned. "I—I don't remember." A slow nod. A couple of blinks. "Oh, I get it. You're suggesting Silver was made into hamburgers." Chris roared with laughter, his sudden shout of merriment making the others laugh even harder.

"I do have a motorcycle here," Mac said. "Somewhere." He looked around then stomped off through some prickly looking bushes.

The others followed, and there under some thick plastic sheeting was a motorcycle leaning against Mac's old redwood fence.

"This was a prop from the 1968 Marianne Faithful movie, *The Girl on a Motorcycle*," Mac said, running a loving hand over the machine as he tore off the plastic cover. "It's a 1967 Harley-Davidson Electra Glide. They sure don't make 'em like this anymore."

"Does it work?" Jhonny asked.

"Not for decades, as far as I know. I got it cheap because the engine gave out."

"I can make it work." Chris moved forward and ran his

hands over the motorcycle. Within seconds, the engine roared to life."

"What the fuck just happened?" Mac asked, sloshing lemonade everywhere. "My fucking God. It's running. Without a key."

Chris slid his hands over the motorcycle again. "I don't know why you want a key. You just need to stroke it like I am, and it'll start."

Mac gave a sort of weird giggle then tried it. The engine came back to life. A swipe in the opposite direction, and it stopped again.

Chris looked pleased with himself, but Mac tottered back the way they'd come, a sick look on his face.

The others followed but wandered off toward more signs.

"My God. I never thought I would live to see the actual Schwab's Pharmacy sign." Darren stared up at it from its perch in a bed of morning glory vines on a long, tall trellis.

"Sure. And look over here. These are some of the original soda fountain bar and stools," Jhonny said.

"Dang. It all makes me hungry," Darren said.

"Yeah. And you know what? I could use another lemonade," Jhonny said. They turned around. As they made the trek back toward Mac, Chris suddenly pulled at Ever's shirt, tugging him between a thick cluster of birds of paradise.

"Ever, I must have you," he murmured, his voice hypnotic and deep. "I long to pleasure you."

Before Ever could respond, Chris's mouth was on his throat. Ever's breath caught, hard, and his mouth yearned for immediate contact with the man who quickly had Ever's cock leaking in his vintage jeans.

"Oh, fuck," he whispered into Chris's mouth.

"Exactly what I had in mind." Chris's voice rumbled deep against Ever's mouth as he opened the buttons on Ever's fly. They both moaned as Chris's fingers made contact with Ever's cock.

"God . . . what the hell is happening to me?" Ever ground out. "I'm never like this."

"I like you this way, but I like you even better naked, flat on your back, with my tongue buried deep inside your ass."

Oh, shit. Ever almost came on the spot.

"Don't waste it," Chris warned. "I want to make you come hard."

His hand on Ever's cock was too much to take. He stroked and jerked, his mouth moving over Ever's face and . . . holy crap . . . he lifted Ever's T-shirt, and his mouth closed over his nipple. Chris sucked at Ever, whose senses spiked.

"I'm gonna come, Chris. I can't help it."

Chris immediately released him, bending down to suck Ever into his mouth.

Ever gripped the man's head and he fucked Chris's face. He hoped he wasn't gonna make the guy gag, but he was close to coming. Oh, man. Chris's tongue worked under Ever's cock head, taunting the ridge and vein pulsing there. Ever stood on his toes as he started to come, hard, deep and totally blissed-out. He was still coming when Chris eased him to the ground. He sucked Ever until he finally stopped shooting.

"Where are you?" Jhonny called out.

He was so close, Ever couldn't pretend not to hear him.

"Be right there," he shouted back. He felt the loss of Chris's wanting, sucking mouth on him as soon as he sat up. He took Chris's face in his hands.

"I owe you one, and I promise you, I'll make it up to you."

"Yeah, you will," Chris said. His expression turned mournful. "I love licking you until you come."

Ever gulped. He didn't think he could wait. But he had to. Chris helped him to his feet as Ever tucked his cock back into his jeans.

"I like this," Chris said, planting a kiss on the still raging, hard shaft.

"It likes you, too. A lot."

"You kill me," Jhonny whispered across their booth at Crazy Pie. "Good for you having a quickie between the tikis. Chris seems so hot for you, bro." He clinked soda glasses with Ever. Jhonny had never seen his best friend look so happy or . . . satisfied.

"It was fun." Ever grinned.

"He's a little wacky though, dude, but I gotta say, giving his clothes up to a homeless man . . . I kinda liked that." He paused. "How the hell did he start Mac's motorcycle?"

"I forgot to ask. I was too busy getting my own engine taken care of." Ever grinned. "I need to talk to him about that. Hey, Vanessa."

Vanessa came by their booth at the same moment that Chris and Darren came out of the john.

Jhonny couldn't fail to notice the frisson of attraction between his sister and Darren.

"Hi, beautiful." Darren's gaze remained on her long after a red-faced Vanessa deposited their menus and walked bang-slap into a wall as she returned to the kitchen.

"She's beautiful," Darren said, watching her walk away.

"She's my sister."

Darren flicked a glance at Jhonny. "No shit? Wow. Can you introduce me?"

Over lunch of pizza and salad, Jhonny watched the way Darren drew his sister out of her shell. He'd never seen her smiling so much.

"You mind if I take her to the movies with her friends Saturday instead of you?" Darren asked Ever after returning from an alleged trip to the restroom.

"Not at all. Go for it."

Chris was acting a little weird. He kept commenting on the restaurant's décor and how the ancient Egyptians had invented the first pizza.

"Only it wasn't called pizza," he said. "It was usually sweet, too, since we ground our wheat by hand and poured honey over it."

Everybody stopped eating.

"We?" Ever asked.

Chris didn't have a chance to respond. Vanessa arrived with four gigantic slices of Italian caramel cake.

"You guys are my guinea pigs," she said, her gaze on Darren. "Something I've whipped up for the dessert menu."

Jhonny slid his fork into the moist cake. He swallowed a generous bite.

"God, sis, you can cook," he said. The others just moaned.

"This is the finest cake I ever tasted," Chris declared. Vanessa lit up when Darren stood and kissed her cheek.

"You're better than Martha Stewart," he said.

Jhonny caught Ever's gaze. He knew that, like Jhonny, Ever wanted nothing more than Vanessa's happiness.

She giggled and ran off to the kitchen, avoiding the wall this time. She seemed a hundred years younger than she had that morning.

Ever reached across the table, touching Jhonny's hand. "You heard from Mike Fletcher today?"

Jhonny shook his head.

"Call him . . . see how the audition went."

Jhonny balked at the idea.

"Can't hurt," Ever insisted.

Jhonny hated chasing after guys. He sighed, pulling his cell phone out of his pocket. Before he could make the call, he received one. From Mike. He couldn't keep the smile from his face.

"Hey," he said. "How did it go?"

"Damned fine. Listen, they loved me here at the studio. They just gave me half a dozen passes to the Universal Studios tour for free. We can go on rides and take the tour as well. They're good for today only. Wanna come meet me?"

Jhonny ran the idea around the table.

"There's four of us," he informed Mike.

"Cool, I'll meet you out front by the ticket booths."

"Maybe we shouldn't have eaten lunch first," Ever said.

Jhonny shook his head. "These rides are nothing like Disneyland."

"Dude . . . you been on the rides there lately? They're pretty intense."

"I'll take my chances."

"Me, too." Darren stood. "Lemme just go say goodbye to Vanessa first."

Mike stood waiting for them in the sun. While the rest of the country was in the middle of abnormally deep freeze temperatures, LA was in the midst of uncharacteristic heat for late January. Uncharacteristic that is, for anyone who hadn't been in town for the devastating Northridge earthquake seventeen years ago. Most locals thought of these balmy, winter days as earthquake weather. In fact, since the last big earthquake in January 1994, Universal had toned down its promotion of its Earthquake: The Big One ride. It simulated an 8.3 magnitude earthquake and was fun and freaky if you hadn't experienced the real thing. Universal had quietly folded the ride into part of the studio tour.

Darren and Vanessa seemed happily a deux, so much so, that Jhonny kept staring at them. His sister never took time off work, and he wondered how his mother was coping with the afternoon crush. No time to think about that now. They split off into pairs as they passed through security and had their tickets scanned. They ran down the pathway to take the studio tour.

"Don't you think it's amazing," Ever said in Jhonny's ear, "that each of us is with the one person we want to be with?"

"Yeah." Jhonny felt his spirits lift. None of the rides had long lines, but they had voted to start with the tour. The guide handed them all pairs of 3-D glasses for the *King Kong* portion of the ride.

Jhonny stood close to Mike, who was a little distracted texting and calling his agent and manager.

"Wow, I wish my daughter was here," Darren said. "She would really dig this."

"You have a daughter?" Vanessa's gaze seared into Darren, who stared at the ground looking woebegone.

"Yeah. She's wonderful. I can't wait for you to meet her."

"How old is she?" Vanessa's expression might well have screamed, *Beam me up a ready-made family, Scotty.*

Darren looked up, his face soft and moony. "She's five. Her name is Ivy —"

"Ivy! Oh, that's a wonderful name. I bet she's a beautiful little girl."

Jhonny was surprised to see Darren growing emotional. "She *is* beautiful."

"She must be in school today." Vanessa took his hand, and it seemed to comfort him.

He nodded. "It's her maternal grandmother's turn to have her. My ex-wife walked out on us when Ivy was a baby."

"No!" Vanessa was aghast. "How could she do that?"

"Drugs." He looked down at the ground again. "I have full custody, but I let Shannon, that's Ivy's grandma, have her one night a week. Tonight's her night. I already miss my girl though. I hope you like kids . . ."

His voice trailed away. He looked utterly miserable.

"I adore kids."

Darren lifted his head, and the sun came back out again. They kept grinning at each other.

A granddaughter! Oh boy. Mom's gonna go nuts over Ivy.

Jhonny shook himself from his ridiculous reverie and glanced over at Mike.

"What's wrong?" he asked.

"I've got to get this job," Mike said. "I made the stupid mistake of posting all about the audition on my Facebook page. If I don't get it, I'm gonna feel like such an ass."

"You'll get it." Jhonny nodded emphatically.

"Thanks." Mike appeared genuinely pleased by Jhonny's show of support, and he was so damned sexy. Jhonny longed to ask him if he'd been letting other guys blow him at the bowling alley, but this wasn't the time or place. Unfortunately, Mike was agitated, totally stressed out not knowing if he'd landed the soap opera job or not, and he kept glancing at his cell phone. Jhonny, like many of his friends, had made a lifelong policy of not dating actors. He hadn't realized Mike was one. He hated the constant mood swings, insecurities, and uncertainties that being an unemployed, desperate actor entailed, and he wasn't so sure he wanted to be part of the manic ride now.

"Maybe I should call my attorney." Mike mused on this as they climbed into the tram for the start of the tour.

Jhonny wanted to ask about which show Mike had auditioned for, but his attention was on the moment. He was impressed with how much the trams had improved since he last took the tour. The guide was funny and sat facing them, an HD monitor to his right, depicting scenes from famous movies shot right in the various spots where the tram stopped. They approached the creepy *Psycho* house with the skeleton of Mrs. Bates swinging in her rocking chair in an upper window.

"Oh no!" the tour guide shrieked, pretending to be frightened. They paused outside the decrepit Bates Motel as tumbleweed blew past them.

"There's somebody in there," the guide muttered.

"Norman Bates" came out of one of the rooms carrying what appeared to be a body in his arms.

"Norman's" eyes widened as he spotted the tram's occupants. He stalked over to his old Studebaker, dumping the body into the open trunk. As the tram driver pretended not to be able to restart the vehicle, "Norman" came after them with a big, gleaming butcher's knife raised high.

Mike watched the guy, mesmerized.

Some of the kids in the tram squealed. "Norman" got close but suddenly, the tram restarted and they went on, into a Mexican town that became engulfed in a storm, splashing them all with water. They ricocheted through the Wisteria Lane set from the TV series *Desperate Housewives*. The tour was a gas until they came to the 3D portion narrated on screen by movie director, Peter Jackson, whose *King Kong* monster interacted with 3D dinosaurs from *Jurassic Park*. The effects were dazzling, with Kong and the dinosaurs appearing to lunge at the tram occupants. Jhonny was impressed with how real they were, even to rain and dinosaur spit hitting him in the face. He heard manic screaming and realized when everybody in front turned around to stare that it was coming from Chris, who went into a total state of panic. Everybody watched the freaked out guy going nuts, trying hard to escape from the tram.

"He's going to eat me!" Chris screamed. "He wants to eat my brains!"

Even small children on the ride weren't carrying on the way he was. It took Vanessa and Ever sitting on him to keep the guy inside the tram.

He moaned pitifully the rest of the way. People kept turning to stare at him, the tram guide keeping a nervous eye on him. Chris stayed quiet and seemed fine once the ride was over.

"It was so real," he said. "Soooo real." He shook his head. Privately, Jhonny thought the effects were cool, but sheesh . . .

Chris insisted he wanted to go on another ride and soon everyone forgot his amateur theatrics as they went on the *Shrek* ride. Chris even laughed at the four-dimensional ride with wild and wacky sensations of Donkey sneezing on him and spiders crawling over his legs . . .

And then came the *Revenge of the Mummy* ride.

They stood in line on a conveyer belt that moved upward. Everybody chatted excitedly about the impressive recreation of an Egyptian pyramid and temple.

"It's awesome," Ever said. He glanced at Chris, whose head hung down now as if his earlier histrionics on the studio tour had worn him out.

A man's voice came out of a machine as they moved up toward the ride, the images of a ghostly mummy and some kind of pharaoh moving on a monitor.

"Imhotep!" the man intoned. "Imhotep!"

Chris gasped. "Where is he? Where is he?" He tried climbing over the railing, the others forced to hold him back. A fresh surge of passengers drew up behind them. There was no way to get him off the ride at this point.

"Is he this way?" Chris asked, suddenly dropping to his knees, bowing and scraping.

"For God's sake," Ever muttered, reaching down to pick him up by the arm. "Get off the fucking ground!"

They moved forward, all light gone as they advanced into inky darkness. Jhonny saw the image of scarabs skitter across an arch above their heads. He gave himself up to the psychological thrill of the ride as they boarded the roller coaster. They were buckled in, their seat bar barely holding them in as they began coasting through a sinister maze of Egyptian artifacts, mummies looming over them. Then a sudden chill enveloped them as they peered into the empty tomb of Imhotep.

Wispy smoke drifted around them, and then a man's voice came out of a wrapped mummy figure. "Are you insane? Get out of here! The curse is real! This whole place is a trap! He is after your souls! Look for the *medjai* symbol. It's your only hope!"

Chris screamed, a few kids around them screamed, then Imhotep shouted, "Silence!"

As Chris whimpered beside Jhonny on one side, Ever on the other, he looked like he was going to have a heart attack when Imhotep continued.

"With your souls, I shall rule for all eternity!"

Chris' scream almost deafened him as the roller coaster moved forward in total darkness and they dropped. The roller coaster portion of the ride had them all screaming and laughing. Even Chris got into the spirit of the thing.

"What happened to Imhotep?" he kept asking. "Why did he let us survive?"

Oh, brother.

"He's dead, Chris," Vanessa said, sounding exasperated. "Been dead thousands of years."

"Not that long," he insisted. "And nobody knows exactly where he is buried. His tomb's location is a secret."

Oh boy, Ever's got himself a real lulu with this guy.

They came out of the ride once it ended. They turned a corner of the building and a tall, masked man jumped out at them. Mike, walking beside Jhonny, screamed. Chris jumped forward, picking Mike up by the knees.

"The chosen one. He must be saved!" He tore off with Mike now dangling over his shoulder. The crowd roared with laughter like this was part of the ride. The final thrill. The tall man stood on stilts, his costume that of Anubis, the jackal-headed Egyptian god.

Jhonny caught the look of fury in the man's gaze. He was being upstaged on his own ride.

"Run!" Ever yelped.

"Help meeeee!" Mike yelled. "Haaaaalp!"

By the time they caught up with them, Mike was throwing up in a trash bin and Chris was calmly sitting on a park bench eating a piece of Indian frybread.

"This is the tastiest thing I ever ate in my whole life." He held up a finger covered in honey and goo. "I saved him from Anubis. He was sent to accompany the chosen one on his journey into the afterlife. But he has yet to be mummified. I protected him."

Chris gave them a weird smile.

"They have carnival food today." He looked ecstatic. "Wanna bite?" he asked Ever.

Ever growled. "What the fuck is up with you?"

"With me? Nothing's up with me? Don't you just love Indian frybread? You know . . . I left my car at the museum. I really should get back."

The others all stared at him. "What?" he asked.

"Your car's at the museum?" Ever said. "You just suddenly remembered that?"

Chris looked befuddled for a moment. "Yeah. I guess. I think I'm supposed to be working today."

"I'll drop you off there," Ever said.

Mike wasn't moving. He still stood, his head bent over the garbage.

"Are you okay?" Jhonny asked him, his hand on the small of Mike's back.

Mike raised his head, looking terrible. "Imhotep has cursed me. He cursed us all."

Oh God, not him, too.

The group split up. Vanessa and Darren stayed for the rides since they'd come in his truck. The other four left with Ever since he had driven them here in the first place. Besides, Darren and Vanessa no longer seemed to want company. In any case, Jhonny didn't feel like going on any more rides.

"We'll come with you," he told Ever, not understanding why Mike kept crying and sniveling.

Back in the car, something weird happened as they approached the museum.

"I don't want to leave you," Chris suddenly said as they pulled into the parking lot.

He put his hand on Ever's shoulder. "Come with me."

"I can't come with you, sweetie."

"Don't leave me here."

Ever gripped the wheel. "I'll see you later."

"You promise?"

"I promise."

Chris leaned in and kissed Ever, then Ever watched Chris saunter over to his car looking a little bit lost.

"What's up with him?" Jhonny asked.

"No idea. What's up with *him*?" He pointed at Mike, who was asleep in the backseat beside Jhonny. No amount of shaking would awaken him.

"Guess we should drop him back at the bowling alley." Jhonny got out of the car and climbed in the front passenger seat.

Ever glanced at him. "What the fuck happened today?"

"I'd like to blame my sister's pizza . . . or maybe the caramel cake."

"Did you see the way Darren fell all over her?"

"What are you suggesting?" Jhonny bristled, then sagged in his seat. "Yeah. I know . . . it's all too weird. Are you really gonna see Chris later?"

Ever shrugged. "I dunno man . . . he's so freaky. One minute he's cool, the next he's screaming like a frickin' prom queen. Listen . . . about Vanessa. I'm happy for her. She's a wonderful woman, but it was like . . . *boing!* Love at first sight."

"Yeah, either that or he's super-duper infatuated with pizza."

Ever laughed. "Maybe he's really hot for her."

Jhonny shook his head. "Unreal . . . sorry. I love her an' everything but she ain't exactly a bombshell."

"Maybe to him, she is."

Jhonny nodded. He turned to look at Mike, whose mouth lay open in a soft snore, his head lolling against the headrest of the backseat.

"I had high hopes for him as well . . ."

"Hey, you can't blame him. Chris ran off with him, and it *was* a big lunch."

Jhonny laughed.

"Wanna find us some music?" Ever asked.

"Sure." Jhonny surfed the radio stations, catching the four o'clock afternoon news. They caught the tail end of a report that shocked them.

" . . . police say they have no idea how the mummy was removed from the exhibit. The case that held the Egyptian mummy that dates back to 400 B.C. remained intact. The Mummies of the World exhibit will be closed until further notice."

"Holy shit," Ever said.

"Isn't that the exhibit Chris has been working on?" Jhonny asked, flipping the dial in search of more news.

"Yeah. And you know what? There were two Egyptian mummies I saw . . . one was really weird. I swear the mummy's head was raised like he wanted to escape."

"Don't be crazy. Do you hear yourself?"

"I know it, I know it. But listen . . . you think it's possible that somehow the mummy escaped and somehow . . ." He paused.

"Somehow what?"

Ever looked worried when he gripped the wheel even harder.

"What I was about to say makes no sense. Forget about it."

Their conversation was interrupted by a shrill cell phone ringing. Both men jumped. Mike rose from his stupor as they pulled into the bowling alley. He released a loud belch and took the call.

"Hello?" His voice sounded thick.

A pause.

"I got it! I got it!" he shrieked.

Jhonny turned in his seat as Mike did a happy dance, texting madly with his thumbs.

"You got the part?" Jhonny was ecstatic.

"I got the part. Hang on, I'm posting it on Facebook."

Jhonny resisted the temptation to roll his eyes.

"What soap opera did you get on?" he asked.

Mike glanced up from his cell phone. "Soap opera?"

"Yeah . . . you know. The audition?"

"I'm not going on a soap opera. I auditioned at the studio for a character on the studio tour."

"You did?" Ever and Jhonny asked in unison.

"What character?" Ever asked since Jhonny had fallen silent.

Mike leaned forward. "Gentlemen, you're looking at the new Norman Bates on the *Psycho* set. I take over the part first thing Monday. Which reminds me, I gotta dye my hair brown."

He kept texting with one hand, miming stabbing somebody with the other, a look of maniacal glee on his face.

Geez. He's a loon. The story of my whole fucking life.

Jhonny would have sunk into a manic depressive spiral except as they rolled into the bowling alley parking lot, they found a police vehicle there. Chris was getting out of the car. He came toward them. Ever rolled down the window.

"I lost my ka," he said. "Ever. The ka is gone."

"You lost your . . . car?"

"No, Ever." Chris looked really distraught. "My ka, Ever. My ka."

"Chris," Ever said, his voice coming out in a frightened whisper. "What the hell is going on?"

"I'm . . . I'm . . ." His gaze dropped to the ground.

"He with you?" one of the cops asked.

"Yeah." Ever sounded less than thrilled. The cop nodded, gave the wrap it up signal to his partner and they took off.

"Come on, Chris, knock it off. What the fuck is going on? What are you playing at?"

"Playing?" Chris shifted from one foot to the other. "I don't want to go home," he said, suddenly looking petrified.

"We'll follow you, okay?" Ever asked.

"But I don't remember how to drive. I don't remember a lot of things." Chris's head fell again, his hands covering his face.

Ever and Jhonny exchanged glances.

"How about I drive your car and you tell me how to get there?" Jhonny asked. "Ever can follow in his car. Mike can stay with Ever to keep him company."

Chris glanced up, his eyes shiny with unshed tears. "Yes. I'd like that."

Ever jumped from the passenger seat and walked over to Chris's car.

He gave Ever the thumbs up as the car started and they all rolled out of the lot.

CHAPTER SIX

Ever had never been inside a more depressing apartment in his life. From the outside of Chris's building on Griffith Park Boulevard, it was a nice, leafy, sprawling complex, set off by ornamental cherry trees in its many courtyards. Inside, his unit was small, boxy, and very dark. It felt like a womb and unpleasant one at that. The walls were empty, and things were stacked in boxes. Apart from his big, comfy leather sofa, huge plasma TV and bookshelves filled with brand new DVDs and CDs, there was no other sign of life.

"I bought this a month ago through foreclosure but . . ." Chris's voice trailed away as Mike came out of the restroom. Chris walked around suddenly as if he'd never been inside the apartment before.

"Not much, is it?" he asked.

Ever was so surprised he almost asked Chris why he bought it. Chris came over to him in three strides, covering the space between them and hugging him. Ever's cock hardened against Chris's thigh. *Dang.* He had to admit he had a chemical reaction to the guy that was hard to resist, and although he seemed to be fluctuating in his responses and mental acuity, it seemed to Ever that in spite of his looks, Chris was quite introverted and lonely and possibly, depressed. He could identify with the man's loneliness. LA was a bad place for people who were socially awkward. Ever had been lucky finding Jhonny for a best friend. Maybe Chris's idiosyncrasies would iron out with their influence.

"Don't leave me here," he implored. "I want to help celebrate Mike's new job. And I wanna be with you. Please don't leave me here, Ever."

"Yeah, we need to celebrate." Mike's thumbs poised between texts. The man had not stopped with the manic posts ever since he'd received news he was about to play the movie's first honest-to-God wacko on a daily basis.

Chris looked so happy, turning a pleading gaze on Ever.

God . . . those puppy dog eyes.

"Oh, all right." Ever allowed the other three to cajole him into letting Chris come home with them. They left his car in the building parking lot, Chris claiming to have the next couple of days off.

They drove home, and the weird thing was it seemed perfectly natural to be driving around on a gloriously sunny weekday, with Chris's hand on Ever's lap as Mike and Jhonny warbled away to 'All I Wanna Do is Have Some Fun,' helping Sheryl Crowe on the chorus. Ever badly wanted to listen to the news on the radio, hoping for some fresh info on the missing mummies. However, soon he, too, sang at the top of his voice about hanging out until the sun came out on Santa Monica Boulevard.

"Can I hang out, too?" Chris asked, as soon as the song stopped.

For the first time, Ever realized the guy was a total crackup. He joined the others in laughter, but Chris stared at him. He seemed to be waiting for a response.

"Of course you can," Ever said. Chris's hand tightened, moving up a little higher. Ever's cock responded with, *boing!*

In the once-safe, sanctified apartment Ever shared with Jhonny, Norman Bates and the most emotional security guard on record rehearsed his big acting scene with the body and the car trunk.

Mike kept trying to pick up Chris, who was just too heavy.

"You're going to give Norman Bates a hernia," Jhonny observed. Ever took advantage of their silliness to watch the TV news reports about the missing mummy. It was the mummy he'd stared at in fascination. Nobody could explain the missing remains of the circa 400 BC man the media had inexplicably dubbed 'Max.'

"I like that name," Chris said as he ate his third bowl of Cheerios topped with milk and ice cream.

He and Mike seemed more excited about Mike playing Norman Bates than Jhonny and Ever were. Jhonny took a run.

"Keep an eye on him for me, will you?" he asked Ever. "I've never been so stressed out in my life."

Neither had Ever. *Ever.*

He listened to Mike's dreams, Chris showing enormous enthusiasm. Ever brewed coffee and stared out of the window. Was Chris involved with the disappearance of the mummy? Was he . . . in fact, the mummy? No, he was being fanciful . . . stupid. And Chris couldn't have been involved with the mummy's theft since he wouldn't even take stuff out of Dumpsters, for chrissakes.

Ever felt a hand on his arm and almost hit the ceiling he jumped so high. It was Chris. He gave Ever a sweet kiss on the cheek and smiled.

Dang. Why am I so hot for this cuckoo bird?

"I need some things in the kitchen," Chris said.

"What do you need?"

Ever followed him inside as Chris busied himself opening cupboards, humming a tune that sounded suspiciously like, 'Don't You Want Me?'

"You have so many spices and condiments," Chris said over his shoulder.

Ever stared. "What are you doing with them?"

"Coloring Mike's hair. I always colored the pharaoh's hair."

He walked off whistling. Now that was a sentence you didn't hear every day.

Ever listened to the two men laughing and talking in the living room, arguing about how dark Mike should go.

"I can make a mixture that will last for weeks," Chris said, before rushing back into the kitchen with Mike, whose face glowed. They scooted Ever out of the room. Fine by him. He could keep an eye on the news. However, he soon fell asleep on the sofa, only awakening when he felt a mouth on his cock.

His eyes flew open. The living room was dark, everything was quiet, the only sound was Chris's insistent sucking. He knelt on the floor beside him, holding Ever's cock through the open buttons of his fly with reverent fingers, his mouth coming off him for a moment.

"Been dying to do that all day," Chris said. "Mike and Jhonny went to bed. You want to continue this here or in our bed?"

Our bed? Ever might have protested these words but a hot mouth and his own hard cock delivered him from his senses.

Chris began a fresh, relentless assault on Ever's cockhead, crooning as his tongue lapped at Ever's syrupy juices.

"Bedroom," he gasped, loving the way Chris got such pleasure out of giving head.

"I was hoping you'd say that." Chris grinned and got to his feet, carrying Ever to the darkened bedroom.

He threw him onto the bed, making Ever laugh.

"Wait," he said, pushing Chris back. "I've got a surprise for you."

Chris frowned. "What do you mean? What kind of surprise?"

"It's in the bread bin in the kitchen."

"I'll get it. You stay there. I don't want you moving a muscle out of this bedroom now that I've finally got you where I want you."

Ever grinned. "Okay. It's in a white paper bag. No peeking. Okay?"

"Sure." Chris shrugged and left the room, returning a minute later. "Okay, I cheated. I looked. It's some kind of sticky bun. I don't get it. What's the surprise?"

He looked so disappointed, Ever reached up for a kiss.

"It's a pecan snail bun. One of my favorites. Chris, have you ever had a pecan mummy?"

"A . . . pecan mummy? No . . . I don't believe so."

Ever sat up on the bed, taking possession of the bag.

"Get naked. We're going to have fun with food."

"I adore fun with food!"

Chris ran to the bedroom door and locked it. He returned, dropping trou. He must have realized he was in for a very special treat because he was sporting a nice hard-on. He watched with a widening grin on his face as Ever took the pecan pastry, breaking off the outer circle.

Ever smiled up at him. "This part is a little dry to wrap around your cock, but it's still tasty. Want to try some?"

"Sure." Chris reached down for a piece. He ate steadily, watching Ever gently unrolling the gooey, moist inner circles of the bun until he held one long strip of pastry in his fingers. He urged Chris closer. Starting at the base of the man's cock, he rolled the pastry around the shaft all the way up to the head.

Chris gasped. "Oh, man, that feels strangely . . . erotic."

"Good. I've always wanted to try this ever since I saw it in a porn movie. I just gotta be careful I don't break the pastry before I can give you a damned good sucking."

"I adore getting a damned good sucking."

Ever smiled. "And I adore giving them."

Chris's cock twitched in his fingers. Ever had started having dreams about this cock. All he wanted to do was pleasure it, to command it . . . to own it. He put his mouth to the pastry piece wrapped around his lover's cockhead, nibbling at the top portion of the sweet, nutty mixture. He took his time, giving equal attention to the pasty and the delicious cock gradually revealing itself from under its cinnamon-fragrant wraps. He moaned when he finally uncovered the head of Chris's cock. He sucked and licked it, moving his mouth down to the next piece of pastry wrapped around the shaft.

Ever wasn't sure who derived more pleasure from the cock pastry party, him or Chris. But as he worked off another section of the bun and pleasured the final uncovered section of hot male meat, Chris's moans got louder and louder.

Ever sucked and swallowed the beautiful, big cock in his mouth. He didn't stop until he'd finished the entire pastry, teasing Chris with his tongue and tight lips until the man exploded in his mouth.

"Oh, Ever! Oh, *Ever*! Do that again. Do that again!"

Ever reached up for a sticky kiss. "I will, I promise."

"You only bought one?" Chris pouted. How can I reciprocate if you bought only one pastry?"

"It was the only one they had at the bakery, but I promise you from now on, I'll buy them in bulk."

"You'd better," Chris growled.

He fell on top of Ever, their hard cocks colliding.

"This is all I think about now, you know," Chris said, kissing Ever hard.

Ever wrapped his legs and arms around him.

"Me, too, sweetie. I just . . . I can't wait for you to fuck me."

"Oh, I'm gonna fuck you, and I'm not going to stop fucking you until you come hard for me. Think you can do that,

Ever?"

Ever nodded. He was afraid to speak. If he spoke, he was certain he'd say goofy things, like tell the man he loved his cock more than coffee or cake, or air, or . . . or . . . no. It was best to keep his mouth shut and just go for it.

Chris bent his head down to suck Ever's cock and stroke his ass.

"You have the sweetest cock, Ever. I want to suck it all day long."

Ever gave himself up to the sensations of incredible sex with Chris. He couldn't believe their sexual chemistry, and how each time they made love, it got better and better. He loved the way Chris touched him, looked at him . . . and oh, God, the wonderful way Chris fucked him.

A loud knocking on the door later that night roused Ever from sleep. His first thoughts were that Chris was outside mooning the world again, but Chris was still in bed with him, one arm slung around Ever's belly in a tight embrace. The knocking continued. Ever glanced at the clock radio.

Almost midnight. Mrs. Zapel would kill him.

He wriggled out of his lover's grip and threw on some clothes before rushing to the front door. Vanessa fell inside as he switched on lights.

"Oh, Ever, she hates me!"

"Who?" Ever peered over her shoulder, half-expecting to see his landlady, but Vanessa began to pace and rant, her fists clenched in front of her.

"Ivy Moon Stevens. That's who."

"Is that name supposed to mean something? Oh . . ." He scratched his head. "You mean Darren's little girl?"

"What's going on?" Chris was out of the bedroom, naked, until Vanessa covered her mouth with one hand, pointed and giggled with the other. At least it got her happy for a second.

"Be right back." Chris took off and returned in his jeans as Vanessa launched into her story of woe.

"He asked me to come over tonight for dinner. We were having such a nice time, then her grandma called and had to bring her back. I had a Barbie doll just shipped to me from eBay, and it was in the trunk of my car, so I gave it to her."

She screwed up her face, crying. "I wanted us to be friends!"

Ever let her wail in his arms for a moment. She shook him off. He led her inside and shut the front door. He steered her to the sofa, where she dropped her massive purse on the floor.

"I gave her a brand new, mint in box Happy Holidays Barbie doll from 1988 and she acted like I was trying to give her a worm sandwich!" Vanessa huffed. "Do you realize that's *the* most sought-after seasonal release Barbie ever? I've been bidding on that doll for freakin' ever. I finally won an auction, and this is the thanks I get!"

Ever and Chris listened.

"They sell for nearly four-hundred dollars at doll shows, and Ivy Moon Stevens said she doesn't like dolls. *Doesn't like dolls.* What little girl doesn't like dolls?"

"Ivy Moon Stevens?" Chris ventured.

"Exactly." Vanessa pointed at him. "I tell you it's unnatural. *Unnatural!*" she shrieked.

"What's wrong?" Jhonny tumbled out of his room, his hair sticking up all over the place. Mike stood behind him, his hair looking helmet-like.

"I'm going back to bed. I got a long day tomorrow," Mike said as Jhonny joined the others, tying the sash of his bathrobe around his waist.

"What happened, sweetie?"

Ever ran to the kitchen to put the kettle on for tea as

Vanessa repeated her story a little more dramatically this time as her captive male audience of Jhonny and Chris listened.

Vanessa sat on the sofa, waving her arms, crying.

"She hates me. She absolutely hates me!"

"No. Ivy Moon Stevens hates dolls," Chris said. "There's a difference."

"Even if she did, it's not the end of the world," Jhonny ventured.

"It is for me," Vanessa shouted. "How can I be close to a little girl who hates dolls? I never heard of such a thing." She started to wind herself up again, so Ever raced into the kitchen and poured the boiled water into mugs with herbal tea bags in them. He came back out, pressing a cup of chamomile into her hands, hoping it would calm her.

"Look at it this way," Jhonny said, from his perch on the coffee table. "She won't tear apart all those collectible dolls you've been saving for all these years. You said yourself you've been bidding on this one doll for a long time."

"That's true," Ever said.

"But I adore dolls." Vanessa's expression was so mournful it broke Ever's heart.

"Find out what she likes and show some interest in her hobbies," Chris suggested. Ever thought this was excellent advice.

"Oh, I know what she likes," Vanessa muttered darkly. "She—oh, it's too much. I can't." She fell back against the sofa, one arm slung across her eyes.

Chris sat beside her on the sofa, patting her hand between his big paws.

"It's okay, Vanessa. You can tell us."

Ever wondered what she could possibly be into that would create such hysteria in Vanessa.

"She wants to ride bikes. Okay? And she said something

about a go-cart. Do I look like the kind of lady who rides a bicycle for frickin' frick's sake?"

The men were silent for a few seconds before Chris squeezed her hand again.

"But this is perfect. You can get her a pink riding helmet." He turned to Ever and Jhonny. "Say, maybe I can make her a go-cart."

"Fantastic idea!" Jhonny enthused. "I had one when I was a kid."

"And this involves me and makes me look wonderful, how?" Vanessa asked.

"We'll make it, and you can give it to her," Chris said.

Vanessa's mouth fell into an open O.

"Well . . ." She picked at the hem of her shirt, her wounded expression flickering into a small spark of hope. "I guess that could work. You think she'll wear a pink helmet?"

"Ask her daddy what her favorite color is," Chris suggested.

"Purple," Vanessa said. "Her whole bedroom is purple."

"Then she'll have a purple go-cart. Jhonny, we need some boxes, we need some paint and . . ." His voice drifted away as he and Jhonny walked into the kitchen.

"I could look for a purple helmet on eBay," Vanessa said.

"Atta girl." Ever sat beside Vanessa. He put his arm around her, and she relaxed, finally, allowing him to comfort her. He kissed her smooth, glossy hair. She sipped her tea. Her hair smelled like carnations. She always smelled like carnations and pizza sauce.

"Other than the Barbie fiasco, how was your evening?"

"Wonderful." She sipped again. "I want her to like me. Darren's such a nice guy."

Her eyes filled with fresh tears.

"How does he feel about what happened?"

Vanessa grinned at him.

"He said she likes me. He said she used to love dolls until her mom ran off. Maybe those things are related. Maybe not."

"I do know one thing," Ever said.

"What's that?"

"She'd be the luckiest little girl in the world if she winds up having you even remotely connected with her life."

"Oh! Ever! What a nice thing to say!"

She slopped hot tea on his thigh as she reached in for a hug, but he didn't care. Vanessa had a heart the size of a mountain. He'd meant every word he'd said about Ivy.

"Is she beautiful?" he asked.

"Gorgeous." She sat up suddenly and reached for her cell phone out of her purse. "Look!"

She scrolled through her photos, and he was surprised to see a pretty, China doll of a girl smiling into the camera.

"Isn't she spectacular?"

He smiled at Vanessa's doting face.

"Her mom's Japanese. That's another thing. I'm going to have to learn German."

German? Ever had no chance to query this. Jhonny and Chris rushed into the living room to announce they were making a midnight run to Home Depot.

"We need ball bearings. This is gonna be the best, most amazing go-cart ever," Jhonny said.

"Bring us back some ice cream," Ever said.

"Anything else?"

"Yeah." He jutted his chin toward Chris. "Make sure you bring him back with you."

Jhonny laughed, and Chris leaned in for a kiss.

"Just one thing." Chris stopped nuzzling him. "Do you want the go-cart to fly or not?"

The smile froze on Ever's lips, but the others laughed.

"No flying," Jhonny insisted. "Ever . . . if Mike wakes up,

tell him we'll be back soon."

"Okay." Ever returned their finger waves as they walked out the door.

"What a character that Chris is." Vanessa put down her cup. "Wanna watch a movie?"

Ever nodded, but inside, the feelings of panic and dread had started rising high and fast. What if Chris hadn't been joking? What if he really thought he could make a go-cart that could fly?

The next few days proved to be busy ones for Ever and Jhonny. With friends and associates keen to be involved with the new museum project, they rushed back and forth between their home and the proposed space in Hollywood, showing everyone around. Even Darren Stevens and Chris were interested in investing.

"I want to help you get it ready," Chris said when he and Darren inspected the building.

He had great ideas about creating an open-plan second floor, loft-type space. Ever and Jhonny were impressed.

Darren invited them all to dinner the following Saturday.

"It's kind of . . . my birthday," he said, looking embarrassed. "Vanessa's cooking. I also want you to meet my daughter."

Chris had finally been forced to return to work at the bowling alley, even though he railed against the notion. For Ever, it was the respite he needed. He and Jhonny needed to talk shop, though he did enjoy Chris being around. They made plans to see each other that night and Ever frankly looked forward to it, though he wanted to talk to Jhonny about business.

"Thank God Mike's broke," Jhonny said when he and Ever walked into Crazy Pie for lunch. They'd just dropped

Chris at the bowling alley after taking him home to change. His car wouldn't start.

"Why do you say that about Mike?" Ever asked as they slid into their favorite booth.

"You and Chris seem to really dig each other . . . Mike . . . I dunno. I don't feel the . . . you know, the whatever vibe. I don't want to be involved in business with him."

"I understand what you're saying, and I feel the same way. Chris is great, but I want to keep it separate . . . you know the love stuff and work stuff."

"So it's love?"

Ever lifted his shoulders. "You know what I mean. I want to keep it separate like I said. Hey, I can't wait to see this go-cart. You and Chris have been so secretive about it."

Jhonny's face turned dreamy. "Wait until you see it. It's amazing, E. Chris is really incredible with mechanical stuff. I still don't know how he made Mac's motorcycle start without tools or anything. I'm afraid to ask how he did. He just says he has the touch, whatever that is. Who knew?" He glanced around. "Where's Ma? I see other people are waiting, too. It's not like her. I'm gonna head to the kitchen and see what's up."

He slipped out of the booth as Ever said, "What's with the car thing all of a sudden? First, you're without wheels, now Chris."

"Don't remind me," Jhonny griped. "I'm still waiting for the insurance company to pay me so I can buy something. Maybe I should rent a car in the meantime."

"Hey, we can share my car for now," Ever said. "Here's your mom."

Rosa Gallo rushed over with menus, not that they needed them, and a German phrase book dropped out of her apron pocket.

"It's for you," she said, shoving it at Jhonny when he

picked it up off the floor.

"Me? Why?"

"Both of you," she said. "Ivy is in a German immersion school in Glendale. She is taught in German, one hundred percent German. I never heard of such a thing."

Ever grinned. She sounded just like Vanessa.

"We're all going there Saturday night for dinner. She's all excited about the go-cart you and Chris have been making for her. Vanessa bought her a crash helmet. Little Ivy wears it everywhere."

Ever was surprised. "You've met her?"

Rosa put a hand to her chest. "Oh, yes. Oh . . . Ever . . . please pray to all the saints and angels of pizza makers everywhere that my Vanessa doesn't screw this one up. I'm already crazy about that child." She paused. "*Schönes kind.* That's German for beautiful child. And she is. I'm just glad they're not teaching her in Korean. The other mothers at school tell me and Vanessa that language is really tough."

She snatched the menus out of their hands. "The usual, boys?"

Before they could respond, she rushed off, oblivious to the people in other booths trying to get her attention.

Jhonny flicked through the book. "How do you say crazy family in German?" he asked.

"I don't know, but I could try telling you in Korean," Ever joked.

When Saturday rolled around, Chris was strangely nervous about how Ivy would react to the go-cart. Ever was knocked out when he saw the finished product Chris and Jhonny had been hiding in Mrs. Zapel's garage.

"My God," he said, circling the golden-hued machine in the driveway. "Guys, this is exquisite."

"You really think she'll like it?"

"Like it? She'll love it. You've even got ceramic cupcakes for the door handles."

Chris grinned. "Vanessa told me Ivy loves cupcakes." He dropped his voice. "It's ready to fly, too, but I won't tell her how to activate that function until she's older."

Ever felt the blood draining from his body. "Please explain this flight thing."

"Egyptians were the first ones to invent flight craft. And motorcycles. I was the king's machine technician and chief warrior. You call them mechanics here. One day I will build the two of us a motorcycle the likes of which you've never seen."

"Okay." Ever knew it would take time to absorb all of this. He stared at the purple satin seat cushions, the dashboard with the gleaming, golden steering wheel, and the speedometer and emergency brake button.

"I'm having some serious go-cart envy." He hugged the guy. Chris could be so endearing as well as hotter than hot. Even when he said things that were so outlandish. Ever had been so immersed in their new relationship, he'd forgotten about the missing mummy and so many other things.

"Well, I'm glad you like it. I did it for you, Ever." Chris looked pink with pleasure that Ever was so complimentary about it.

"For me?"

"You never ask me for anything, but you give me so much. Ever, when I'm with you, everything else flies out the window."

"Fuck! Me, too. I thought it was just me."

Chris shook his head. "Oh, no. I've got Everitis pretty badly."

Ever threw back his head and laughed.

"Wine," Jhonny suddenly yelled. "We forgot the wine!"

He ran back upstairs.

Ever watched him, smiling. He felt really good. Now, he couldn't wait to meet Ivy. He'd even managed to master a few German greetings to exchange with her. He ran through them in his mind as Chris loaded up the go-cart into the car.

Guten abend, which meant good evening. *Hübsches kleid* for pretty dress. Ooops . . . what if she wasn't wearing a dress? *Pretty pants* wouldn't be the right thing to say. What was the word for pants anyway? Lederhosen?

"What's wrong?" Chris asked as Jhonny came running from the house with the wine they'd promised Vanessa they'd bring to dinner.

"I've forgotten all the German I learned all day to speak to Ivy."

"Don't worry, Ever. I speak fluent German. I'll whisper some things in your ear for you to say."

"You'd do that for me?" Ever asked as they got in the car, Chris beside him, Jhonny in back.

"Sure I will, baby. It will cost you though."

Boing! Ever shifted in his seat.

"What exactly will it cost?" he asked, as he started the car.

"You'll see." Chris winked.

"You two don't need a room, you need a frickin' hose," Jhonny said.

Ever didn't respond. It wasn't his fault that Mike hadn't returned any of Jhonny's calls lately . . . or that Jhonny claimed not to care.

He drove to Darren's house in Studio City. They were the last to arrive. Little Ivy was as adorable as her pictures, and she was out of her skin with excitement to see the new go-cart.

"Look, Vanessa," she kept saying, plucking at Vanessa's hands. Ivy was over the . . . well, moon, when she saw her own special deluxe purple people machine.

"Oh, boy!" She and her dad jumped into it and drove down the street.

Everyone applauded.

"She's so cute!" Rosa kept saying. "Where's my husband? He better not be hiding in his bowling alley reading girlie magazines." She pulled her cell phone from her pocked.

"I'd better go finish dinner," Vanessa said. She sounded very down, which worried Ever. He gave her a couple of minutes and followed her inside.

He was stunned to see she was crying when he found his way into the kitchen.

"What's the matter?" he asked, full of concern.

"I've been in here for hours making a special birthday meal for Darren. I told him he could go to any country in the world he wanted and . . . and . . . he wanted to go to France."

Ever was touched by this. "Okay," he said gently, putting his arm around her. "So what's the problem?"

She howled into his shoulder for a moment then pushed herself away from him.

"I made an appetizer of French quiche from the White House Cook Book."

"Wow . . . that sounds amazing."

"It is." She blew her nose into a linen handkerchief. Ever thought she might be the only person he knew who carried linen handkerchiefs in her pocket. "It's Julia Child's recipe, and it has no cheese. Ivy is allergic to cheese. This is the only recipe I've been able to find that doesn't have cheese and he *loves* quiche. I wanted to make something different."

She pointed to an array of amazing looking dishes on the huge farmhouse table.

"I made individual spinach soufflés and . . . and beef bourguignon and . . . and" —she blew her nose again, tears streaming down her cheeks—"mushroom crepes . . ."

Ever spied the cooling quiche languishing on a wire rack

on the sideboard.

"Vanessa, it all looks amazing. The quiche looks perfect. So what's the problem?"

"Dessert," she wailed. "I found an orange cake recipe from 1932, and I followed it to the letter, but it turned into a candy . . . not a cake."

He hugged her again. "Oh, honey."

"What's going on?" Chris loomed in the doorway.

Ever explained Vanessa's problem.

"He loves cake," Vanessa interrupted. "I have to make him a cake. It's his birthday. But between all the other things I made and sauces I still have to finish, I have no time and . . . and . . . and I'm exhausted."

"I'll make a cake," Chris said.

"You will?" She stared at him. "What kind of a cake?"

"An Egyptian chocolate cake."

"You can do that?"

"Sure." He opened the fridge. "I'll need a few things. You have any cinnamon?"

"A ton of it."

She began opening cupboards, and Chris called over his shoulder. "Put the mixing bowl and the beaters in the freezer."

"Why?"

"This recipe requires that they be chilled before we use them."

"Really?" Vanessa looked enthralled.

Ever offered to help but they shooed him out of the kitchen. Once again, Chris had come to the rescue. Ever heard his soothing tone with Vanessa and her sudden laughter. He felt a huge amount of pride and pleasure that Chris had come to her aid so effortlessly.

I had no idea he could be such an awesome guy.

Ever found Jhonny on his cell phone, grinning away.

"Mike's coming over. He's finished for the day. Isn't that

awesome?"

"Fantastic," Ever agreed. He was relieved to see his best friend looking so happy again.

Rosa rushed inside with her husband, who looked grumpy, and Darren and little Ivy, who ran into the kitchen shouting for Vanessa.

"Did you learn any German?" Rose turned on her husband.

"In the war I did, babe."

"War? What war?"

"The battle of the sexes."

Jhonny and Ever laughed.

"Shhh!" Rosa whispered dramatically. "You can't say the word sex in front of Ivy. I never heard of such a thing!"

Jimmy Gallo frowned at Ever. "What's up with your boyfriend? Did he quit his job? He hasn't been in all week."

This was news to Ever. As far as he was aware, Chris had been working all week.

He didn't have a chance to question Jhonny's dad though. Ivy announced from the living room door that dinner was being served.

Darren asked Ivy to remove her helmet.

"*Nein!*" she shouted.

"What do you mean no?"

"I love my helmet, Daddy!"

"Yes, but we don't wear it at the table, young lady." He reached over to her, and she ran right under the table.

Chris came out of the kitchen with a steaming platter of food. He put it on the table. Every adult in the room stood and listened as Ivy let loose with a couple of fractious *Neins* and then got an attack of the giggles as Chris chatted away with her in what appeared to be rapid-fire German. He led her out again, Ivy clinging to his fingers.

"I love my Chris!" she shouted.

Chris laughed, hoisting her into his arms. He deftly removed her helmet, passing it to Rosa.

If Vanessa was upset that Ivy commandeered Chris's attention all night, virtually ignoring her, she didn't show it. In fact, she was in fine form playing Martha Stewart to rave reviews from her fans.

Between them, Chris and Vanessa made the best meal Ever had ever eaten in his life. He and Jhonny kept licking their cake forks, declining extra slices of cake but gobbling them up when their protestations were ignored.

"Dang, Vanessa. You need to open up a gourmet restaurant," Jhonny said. "Your talents are wasted slinging pizza. Don't you think so, Darren?"

Ever winced. He didn't want anyone pushing Darren. This was the closest Vanessa had come to an honest-to-God relationship and one whiff of a *Fatal Attraction,* and she'd be a goner.

"Hell, no," Darren said.

Vanessa's face fell.

Ever wondered who was going to beat the guy up harder, him or Jhonny, but then Darren reached over and grabbed her hand.

"I prefer Vanessa making pizza for the rest of the world, and Ivy and me getting the gourmet stuff for ourselves."

"Uh-huh!" Ivy seconded. "I love my Nessa!"

Vanessa's smile turned goopy.

"And our friends and families . . . sometimes." Darren grinned around the table.

Chris smiled at Ever, who smiled right back. Everybody else laughed. Jhonny sat in stunned silence. He glanced over at Ever.

"Nice save," he whispered. Ever squeezed his roommate's shoulder. Maybe, just maybe, all of them were finding their romantic way at last.

Chris meanwhile seemed pleasantly tipsy as he sipped more wine and accepted praise for his fabulous cake.

"Thank you, thank you," he said, slurring his words. Then suddenly, "Mike's coming."

Ever glanced at him. "How do you know?"

"I recognize his scent."

What the fuck? Ever's blood chilled, the food he'd inhaled turning into rock in his belly.

The front doorbell rang. Ivy ran off with Jhonny to answer it.

"My Jhonny!" he heard her squeal.

People began moving their chairs to accommodate the new arrival.

Ever couldn't take it anymore. He leaned across to Chris. "What the hell are you playing at?"

"I'm not playing." Chris stared at him. "I hope to be playing with you later. I have plans for your fine ass, my friend."

Ever gulped as the others kept talking. It was his last chance before they all took their seats again.

"Who the hell are you?" he hissed at Chris.

"I am me." Chris sipped his wine. Ever feared what was about to come next. He didn't know what to expect, but it wasn't the response he got.

"My dear Ever," Chris intoned in a pompous way, hand on his heart, "I am the love god."

The others stopped speaking when Ever asked, "Love god?"

"Yes, the love god of Indian frybread. I am the love god of Indian frybread, and I want my ka. Vroom vroom."

CHAPTER SEVEN

His ka.

"His car?" Little Ivy asked, gazing at the adults around her. "And what's Indian frybread?"

"Very tasty stuff," Chris assured her.

She gave him a wonderful smile that dazzled Ever. The kid had charm to spare.

Everyone else meanwhile, talked at once.

"No more wine for you, mister," Vanessa kidded, elbowing Chris in the ribs.

Mike produced his Norman Bates knife and pretended to terrorize Ivy, chasing her around the room.

Typical actor, can't stand to have the attention away from him. Ever watched as the little girl ran around the room play-screaming, making the others laugh. But Ever gulped.

His ka. Okay. Don't panic. There's a logical explanation for this and now is not the time or place.

Ever felt beads of sweat on his forehead and upper lip. He longed for the appropriate moment to excuse himself so they could leave. He and Chris needed to have a serious talk. Ivy's screaming and mad laughter started to wear on him. Chris joined in the game, Ever and Jhonny watching from the table.

"I'm thinking he really believes he is Norman Bates," Jhonny said, leaning closer to Ever. "Why's he still in costume? And do you see the glassy look in his eyes?"

Oh, great. My boyfriend could possibly be possessed by a thousand-year-old mummy and Jhonny's by a fictional, homicidal maniac.

"Jhonny, we need to talk," Ever said.

"Sure, sure." Jhonny craned his neck to watch Mike.

Ever felt Chris's hand on his shoulder.

"I think I want to go home," Chris said. "I think maybe I ate too much cake."

Cake? How about all that booze, buddy?

Ever merely nodded.

"I'll stay," Jhonny told him, wiggling his eyebrows. "Maybe Mike'll let me get lucky tonight."

Ever was frankly relieved. He wanted to talk to Chris . . . wanted to assuage his ridiculous beliefs . . . and have a good laugh when Chris explained what the fuck a ka was.

Ivy wept hot tears as they tried to leave. Chris cuddled the little girl in his big arms, murmuring to her soothing words in what Ever assumed was German.

"*Gehen nicht!*" She sobbed, reaching over for Ever to hold her. "*Gehen nicht!*"

"What did she say?" Ever asked Chris.

"She doesn't want us to go."

"We're going," Ever said, firmly.

Vanessa took Ivy into the kitchen to distract her. Ever felt dreadful when he heard the child's wracking sobs.

"Let's go," he told Chris, who looked upset.

"What's wrong, Ever?" he asked as they got into the car.

"We'll talk when we get home."

"That sounds . . . ominous."

Ever gripped the steering wheel. Yeah. It felt ominous, too.

Jhonny watched Mike acting a fool, and tried a couple of times to snatch the big butcher knife out of the guy's hand. Even Ivy had tired of the game. He made contact finally and to his shock, discovered it was no toy knife. It was the real deal. He tried to hide his cut hand and examine it in the privacy of the bathroom, where he hid the damned knife on top of the bathroom cabinet, away from Ivy's reach.

He ran cold water over his hand.

Mike invaded the bathroom.

"Where's my knife?" His eyes glittered dangerously.

Jhonny held out his injured hand. "That's a real knife, doofus. You cut me!"

Mike stared. "Oh, shit. You're bleeding." He bent and examined the wound. "Superficial," he proclaimed. "Now give me the knife."

"I'm not giving it to you." Jhonny started to feel scared. "If Darren finds out you were chasing his kid with a real knife, he'll call the cops, and I wouldn't blame him."

"It's not real. It's semi-real."

"Semi-real?"

"Yes, I bought it at a novelty store. It's part of the new The O.J. Simpson line."

Oh, my God.

"Don't make me tell Mother," Mike said.

Jhonny stared at him. *Oh, shit. He really thinks he's Norman.* His hand stung when he immersed it back under the flow of cold water.

Mike seemed to come to his senses. "There's got be Band-Aids. Here. I found a whole packet of Scooby Doo bandages. Don't you love Scooby Doo?

"I get carried away sometimes. I'm sorry, Jhonny. I'm a bit of a method actor, you know."

Jhonny didn't know how to respond. A few years ago, he'd read actress Shelley Winters's autobiography, and she'd talked about her studies with The Actors Studio in New York. Her peers had been an eclectic bunch, including Marlon Brando and an uppity newcomer named James Dean who showed up to rehearsal for a scene with a real knife. James Dean was a great actor . . .

Yeah. A great, dead *actor.*

"Come home with me," Mike said, leering at him. "Let's blow this Popsicle stand."

So they blew it, driving away, with the others coming outside to see them off.

Jhonny took the opportunity to stash the knife under the passenger seat as Ivy waved tearfully from Jimmy Gallo's arms on the pavement.

"She's such a sensitive little girl, and she so attached to your family already," Mike observed. "I sure hope they aren't rushing into things."

You and me, both. Not that Jhonny said this aloud. He wanted things to work out for Vanessa. And for Ivy and Darren.

"Your dad is fantastic with her. Where's my knife?"

"Under my seat."

Mike stepped on the brakes. "What's it doing under there?"

"It's against state law to drive with a weapon in plain view."

Mike's eyes widened. "I never knew that. Thanks for telling me, sweetie. I'm so excited you're coming to my house."

"Me, too." *I'm thinking of escaping the first chance I get.*

"Wanna hear some music?" Mike asked.

"I'd love that." Jhonny tried to relax as Mike drove, fiddling with his dashboard CD player. He sailed through two red lights and rolled through a stop sign.

Jhonny would have said something except for the sudden, chilling sound of a shower running, what sounded like a knife being thrust and . . . God help him, a woman screaming.

"Hitchcock really didn't want music for the soundtrack of

Psycho," Mike said. "It wasn't until he directed *The Birds* that he managed to eliminate a traditional soundtrack."

Jhonny didn't think he could handle another night of being lectured to about Hollywood film history. He hadn't had the courage to tell anybody that so far, Mike had done little more than lay a few kisses on him. The two date nights they'd had, he had been a one-man audience for Mike's theater of the absurd. Jhonny felt the hairs on the back of his neck prickling as he heard the strange CD unfold in . . . .ugh . . . surround sound. Minimal music heavily laden with spooky sounds and the eerie, unforgettable screams that accompanied *Psycho's* more terrifying moments at a deafening noise level made him want to open the car door and run.

"That's violins, can you believe it? They call the technique screaming violins," Mike shouted over the racket, sailing through another red light.

"Mike—"

"He's a genius."

"Mike . . . this isn't much fun."

"What do you mean?" Mike turned to him, a spiteful look on his face. "This is my work. I must study!" He pressed a garage door clicker, and they drove into a cavernous subterranean space. Mike drove to a spot where he pulled into a slot, pointing to one next to it.

"I get two spaces. Whenever you visit, you can park right next to me. How cool is that?"

Jhonny nodded, trying to surreptitiously kick the knife even deeper under his seat. He wanted to leave. He wanted to run, but he took a deep breath and followed Mike out of the garage to a well-lit lobby. He had no idea where he was from the brief glimpse outside. He glanced up at the bulletin board as Mike opened his mailbox.

North Hollywood. Okay, cool. He was close to home.

Mike seemed to have subscriptions to every gay magazine

in the world, some of them of a fetish nature that left Jhonny feeling very uncomfortable.

"You're into Japanese shibari rope play?" he asked. His mouth felt dry.

"Oh, yeah. And I can't wait to rig you and fist you."

Jhonny gaped at him, tossing the armfuls of magazines he'd been holding onto the floor. He ran for the front door, panicking when Mike ran after him. Jhonny ran down the street, not sure where he was heading. He took off against the lights, narrowly missing being run down by a truck. The driver honked him, but Jhonny kept running, all the way to Crazy Pie. He kept turning around, but he'd lost Mike a few streets before. Still, he didn't stop running until he reached the kitchen, the staff all staring at him as he collided with a wall unit filled with saucepans.

"That was fast," one of the kitchen hands said. "We only just called your mom and told her we're in trouble."

Jhonny gasped for air, clutching his heart. He really needed a better exercise regime. "Trouble?"

"Yeah. The restaurant's packed, and . . . we've run out of sauce and . . . everything!"

"Packed?" He was trying to follow the conversation, but all he could hear was the damned *Psycho* soundtrack reverberating in his brain.

"Yeah. Didn't you notice when you came in? You got any idea how to make the sauce?"

Sauce. Jhonny could handle that. He was safe in his mom's nice, warm, wonderful kitchen. Plenty of knives on hand if Mike turned up and he needed a handy weapon. His mom always kept them sharp. Besides, he'd been making pizza sauce since he was a kid. He threw on an apron and grabbed a couple of large skillets.

"She was supposed to be back by now. We called, and she said she was on her way."

"How far behind are we?" Jhonny asked.

"Not bad. Three pizzas waiting. We got enough sauce for those."

A waitress ran in with a new ticket. The kitchen staff all looked jittery. Jhonny's mom and Vanessa never took off at the same time. He felt bad for his mom that she had to cut the fun short, but now he was here, he could help. He grabbed tomatoes, spices, and onions and began chopping. He knew his mom added her surprise ingredient of sugar when nobody was looking. He also knew it was hidden in a spice bottle.

"What's on the new ticket?" he asked as he reached for it. He sniffed. Yep. Sugar.

"White pizza with clams."

"You can handle that?"

"Yep."

Jhonny chopped and sautéed. He rolled a couple of garlic cloves under his palm. God, it had been so long, but he was surprised he remembered everything the way his mom did it.

"How are we doing on pizza dough?" he called out.

"Got enough for six pizzas. Benny's mixing some now," somebody shouted.

"Cool."

Jhonny's calm confidence seemed to infuse a little normalcy in the kitchen.

"What's her secret ingredient?" somebody else asked.

Jhonny grinned. "I'd tell you, but I'd have to kill you."

Everybody laughed, and somebody turned up the radio. Sheryl Crowe. That song of hers was turning up a lot lately, and he liked it. Kind of an omen. Jhonny had two big pots of pizza sauce simmering by the time Rosa turned up. The look on her face was priceless.

"Jhonny." She took his face in her hands and kissed his

cheeks. She taste-tested his offerings and grinned. "Perfect."

He grinned. "What else can I do?"

"You wanna help out front? You know how good you are with the customers, Jhonny."

"Yeah, and I know when I'm being played, Mom."

"No, no."

He kissed her cheek. "Yes, yes."

She grinned. He hadn't seen her look so happy in a long, long time.

"Well, maybe a little. Now go. Be the happy host." It didn't surprise him when she turned down the radio. It was just like old times. Out on the floor, he greeted patrons, met a couple of hot guys and collected dirty dishes. He'd forgotten the exhilaration and the reward of feeding hungry people. He tried to remember what it was that he'd hated so much about the restaurant business before. He couldn't. He flirted, chatted and laughed and even collected a couple of phone numbers. He stopped being worried about Mike showing up and even considered one guy's request for a date.

"I'll call you," he said, not trusting his instincts. He thought about calling Ever and asking him for a ride, but decided he'd hang out a while longer and catch a ride with his mom. In the kitchen, she made him coffee, and he remembered how much fun she could be.

"This is so nice," she said, making him sit for a few minutes. "Here, have a little shot."

Oh, boy. He'd forgotten about the hazelnut liqueur she used on special occasions and moments of high stress.

"You okay, Mom?"

She nodded, punching something into her cell phone.

"We need a big delivery tomorrow. I keep forgetting to order things. Ever since your sister met Darren, both our brains have fallen out the window."

Jhonny grinned. "He's a cool guy, isn't he?"

His mom glanced over at him. "Yes, he is. And I really think he likes our Vanessa."

"He really does, Mom. It's awesome."

Her cell phone chirped. "Oh, how cute, Ivy's text-messaging me. Aw ... she misses me." She began texting back, reciting her words aloud. "I miss you, too."

Jhonny excused himself and returned to the front of the restaurant. His own cell phone rang. He checked the readout. Ever. *Call me.*

Ever left a message for Jhonny. He didn't know what to say. He simply texted, *Call me.* How did he confide his worst fears that would sound totally fucking crazy to *anybody,* even himself? Would Jhonny think he was nuts?

He kept thinking about Chris saying he was the love god of Indian frybread. Not that he believed that nonsense ... but was thinking he'd been invaded by the spirit of an ancient Egyptian mummy any less preposterous? What did he really know about Chris? Ever glanced over at him. He lay sleeping on the sofa, a goofy grin on his face. The guy had fallen asleep the moment they got into the car. He'd woken up long enough to stagger up the stairs but was now out ... some guys were happy drunks. Some were aggressive drunks. Chris Coelho was the sleepiest drunk Ever had met in his whole life.

Ever sat at the dining room table beside the sleeping Chris, tapping his fingers against the keys of laptop as he fired it up and went online.

Make a list. That's what I can do. Make a list of why I think he's the mummy. God ... a mummy. What's wrong with me? How can I think he's a dead person? It's ridiculous!

It occurred to him he'd forgotten to check on the museum's missing mummy. MSNBC led with two Egyptian stories. The political riots and to his amazement, the mummy. It had just been found . . . inexplicably in a display case with a mummified cat. How weird. Nobody could explain it since the two mummies were centuries apart in terms of their dates of death.

The mummified cat, however, first thought to be Abyssinian, was still considered by some scientists to be Egyptian. A scientist in London said the cat had been mummified and buried alive. A terrible death. Okay, sure. Ever read through the news reports of a theory being floated around that somebody had moved the man's mummified remains to highlight the cat's plight, to prove a point.

"What is the point?" Ever muttered aloud as he read.

In any event, the exhibit had been reopened and was now functioning again, albeit with heightened security.

Relief flooded Ever's system. Chris had nothing to do with the mummy. It was all just a silly idea. He glanced over at Chris and saw his lover's eyes open, his gaze upon his face. How long had Chris been watching him? He felt, absurdly, that Chris could read his mind.

"Hey," Ever said.

Chris grinned, the beauty of his smile sending wondrous signals to Ever's cock.

How can I be so unsure about this guy, yet so turned on?

"Why are you worried?" Chris asked, his voice soft.

"I'm not worried." Even as he said the words, Ever was aware of the nervousness in his tone.

Chris's eyes drifted shut. He turned over, his soft snoring an indication that Ever was off the hook for now. He waited a beat, but Chris slept on. Ever Googled the guy and, apart from a few old tweets and a LinkedIn profile that hadn't been updated in months, the man didn't have much of an online presence. Ever was relieved he didn't appear to have a secret online porn life or that he was a long-lost serial killer. He did have a Facebook account, but his friends on the social networking site were a few security companies, two guys Ever recognized from their small pool of friends, a few police PR sites and, oddly, a fan site for author and former controversial Los Angeles Police Department chief, the late Daryl F. Gates.

Not that this in itself was odd . . . it was just that, well, Chris didn't appear to have any actual friends. And Gates was . . . well, dead.

Ever clicked back to LinkedIn. He checked Chris's resume. He couldn't see much since Ever wasn't a member himself and he would have to sign up and agree to link up with Chris in order to view his statistics.

Instead, Ever took note of the guy's current employment history, which he already knew. Chris Coelho was a hardworking guy who juggled jobs . . . but according to all the sites Ever accessed, he didn't have much of a *life*.

"What's wrong, Ever?"

Ever jumped. Chris was standing right beside him, looking over his shoulder.

"N-n-nothing's wrong, sweetie."

Oh, man, I'm so caught. I'm screwed! How do I close out this screen without him realizing I've been researching him?

"Hey, talk to me," Chris said.

"I . . . er . . . I was just . . ."

Ever realized Chris was staring at his own Facebook page as if he'd never seen it before.

"What's that?"

"Facebook," Ever responded.

"And what does that do?"

"You don't know what Facebook is?"

"Am I supposed to be able to see my own face in it?"

"No . . . not really." *Oh, brother, who the heck is this guy? I know it's the right Chris Coelho. His picture is on here.*

Ever clicked away from the page. "I was reading up on the missing mummy."

"What missing mummy?"

"The dead Egyptian mummy from your exhibit."

"He isn't missing. He was lonely." Chris let loose with a loopy smile. "Then I found you."

"What did you say?"

Chris shrugged. "I found you. I never thought I'd ever get the right opportunity. I feel bad about the cat, though. I had to leave him behind. He was my only friend, you know."

The cat? Oh . . . no. I'm getting a bad feeling here. How the hell did he know about the cat?

"No, I don't know." Ever swallowed. Hard. "Chris . . . what's with the cat? Who the hell are you?"

"Well, there's some dispute about that."

"Excuse me?"

"I didn't receive a proper burial. I was murdered, you know."

"What? Would you stop saying *you know* when it's obvious I don't know!"

"You've forgotten." It was a flat statement. But Ever felt the weight of disappointment in those two little words. It was like having a conversation with his mother, for chrissakes. Ever couldn't believe what he was hearing. He would have probed further except that Chris yawned and walked over to the sofa, sitting on the edge. He swung his legs up to the cushions.

Oh, no. He's gonna take another nap. I can't let that happen. I have to find out just who the hell he is. It's now or never . . . he'll either freak me out or . . . he'll think I'm the freak and walk out of here.

His palms sweated. He rubbed them against his jeans as he repeated his words. "Chris, who are you?"

Chris leaned back, one arm under his head. "Who am I? That's an interesting question. Sure you want the answer?"

Ever stared at him. The whole world seemed to stop. Ever nodded, even though he was pretty certain he didn't want to know.

"My name is Ammon. Bes Ammon. I was the chief high priest of the spiritual house of the pharaoh, Pi Di Amen."

"Pi Di Amen?" Ever felt faint.

"Yes, Ever. Pi Di Amen."

"Why couldn't it be P. Diddy?"

"Who?"

"Never mind. And you've been dead . . . how long?"

"I died a long, long time ago. How long have I been alive is a more revealing question."

"Oh, my God."

Ever gripped the edge of the table. He was afraid he'd fall over in a faint. "I can't believe what I'm hearing."

Chris stared at him, not saying anything.

"So what happened to Chris Coelho?" Ever asked. "If you're this great temple priest, where the hell is Chris?"

"He's still here. Sort of . . . I mean, let's face it. You've seen his profile. He has no friends, no life . . . nothing. No soul."

"Oh, hell!"

"No. On the contrary. I think he's in Heaven. He's very happy. His body was easy to invade. He wanted you. Without me he had no chance, right? Now he does. You do still like me, don't you, Ever? Look at me . . . look at how we are together. My feelings for you have turned me into a love god. This is all . . . you know, okay with you, isn't it? Even though there's, you know . . . a bit of an age difference?"

Ever laughed in spite of himself. "An age difference?"

"What's going on?"

Ever jumped. He turned to find Jhonny standing in the doorway.

"Jhonny!" He'd never been so happy to see another human being.

"Hey, kid." Chris gave him a little finger wave, lay back and yawned.

"What's he talking about an age difference?" Jhonny

asked, looking confused. He walked in, closing the door behind him.

"Nothing," Ever said. How the hell could he explain Chris's insanity to Jhonny? He'd just get rid of the guy and never, ever see him again.

They could move. To another apartment. Another city. Another country, for chrissakes. He'd heard New Zealand was a nice place.

"Ever?"

"Hmmph?" He twitched when Jhonny touched his arm.

"What's wrong?"

"How do you feel about New Zealand?"

Jhonny stared at him.

"Oh, Ever. You can't run away from this. I'm here now. Why aren't you happy?" Chris asked, sitting up again.

"Don't tell me he's acting freaky, too," Jhonny said.

Ever frowned. "Who else is acting weird?"

"Mike Fletcher. Didn't you see him tonight?"

"Oh. I thought he was just being a big ham."

"Yeah. With a real knife."

Ever gaped at Jhonny's hand. "Man, he really cut you!"

"Yeah. For starters." He gestured toward Chris. "What about him?"

"I thought he . . . I though . . . oh, never mind." Ever flapped his hand.

"He's upset because I took over Chris's body."

Oh God, this isn't happening. It's not!

"What'd you say?" Jhonny stared at Chris.

"I thought you'd understand, Jhonny. You of all people." Chris sounded sulky and hurt.

"What the hell are you talking about?"

"I'm talking about you and me and . . . him." Chris pointed at Ever. "Don't you remember the Ouija board sessions?"

Jhonny and Ever looked at each other and back at Chris.

"The Ouija board?" Jhonny bit his bottom lip. He seemed

deep in thought. "Geez . . . that was a long time ago."

Ever hunted through his own memories. He recalled a couple of strange months where for many nights in their teen years they'd drunk too much Beaujolais and thought they'd contacted genuine spirits through the Ouija board. They were young, stupid and, frankly, petrified when they made contact with—

"Holy shit!" Jhonny shouted. "No! It can't be!"

"Yes! Yes!" Chris jumped up and down, excited. "It's me! You remember!"

"Best Man?" Jhonny asked, his voice a frightened whisper.

The world stood still again. That was the name they'd understood from the board. They thought it was a game. Ever realized now they'd misunderstood and what they thought was Best Man was *Bes Ammon*, the name Chris had mentioned earlier.

"It's me, Bes Ammon," Chris announced with pride. "My name means hidden protector. I was a motorcycle warrior in ancient Egypt, and I was murdered by the king's enemies so I couldn't protect them." His face darkened. "They poisoned me and took my motorcycle. I will rebuild it. For Ever, and for me."

Ever shook his head and walked out the front door. Crap. It was the middle of the night, and it was damned cold. He didn't feel like walking, and nothing was open anyway. There was only one place he could go. The little office he and Jhonny maintained at the back of Mrs. Zapel's property.

He let himself in with the key they always hid in a fake rock outside the door. It might have been unwise but the room from outside looked abandoned, and that was the way he and Jhonny liked it. He let himself in, switched on a light and closed the door.

Ever spent a lot of time working here. Amongst all the

boxes and stuff he and Jhonny kept here, there was also a trusty desktop computer that took the brunt of their flurries of creative inspiration. He turned on the banker's lamp and switched on the monitor. He was nervous but resigned to whatever he might find.

As the computer loaded up, he opened a filing cabinet looking for the notes he had taken so many years ago during what he had come to think of as the channeling sessions with Best Man. Nothing. He could have sworn they were in here. He'd look again in the morning. Maybe when his brain was less fatigued, and he was less emotional.

He went online and Googled Pi Di Amen. There wasn't much information about him. History buffs seemed much more interested in the earlier pharaohs, but the little he did find out about Pi Di Amen was that he had been a black pharaoh. Hadn't they all been black? Ever scrolled through the information. He'd ruled around 400 B.C., which tied in the timeline of the mummy back at the museum exhibit. Amen had apparently built a model glider to conduct experiments in flight.

Amen's leadership came, apparently, after the big era of Vimana Aircraft in Ancient India, Egypt, and Atlantis. Their existence was contested by some scholars, fully endorsed by others.

Ever believed that aircraft probably did exist and it explained a lot. No wonder Chris laughed every time he saw something on TV about planes. They were nothing new to him.

I had no idea that ancient Egyptians knew anything about flight! He wasn't lying to me!

He pulled a legal pad out of his desk drawer and made notes.

To his amazement, he learned that hundreds of years before Amen's rule, the Egyptians had already invented gunpowder for use in their temples and mystery schools. Pi Di

Amen advocated weaponry training and . . . security.

Oh, boy. Gun nut Chris Coelho met his spiritual match when Bes Ammon came a-knocking for a host body.

Ever couldn't find much more about the pharaoh except one interesting footnote in a scholarly journal.

Pi Di Amen had one of the earliest high courts in ancient Egypt, which heard judicial cases every month. For these occasions, he wore a golden wig, which members of the ruling class began to wear instead of the elaborate headdresses previously favored by their culture.

Ever sat back in his chair, grinning. He opened his bottom desk drawer, removed a shot glass and poured himself some Sambuca. He kept the liqueur on a shelf next to his desk. He dropped three coffee beans into the liquid, hunted for matches and lit the drink. The slight roasting of the beans always added to the richness of the flavor. He sipped, feeling better than he had for days.

Now it made sense why Chris went berserk when he saw Mike Fletcher's blond hair and thought people were trying to hurt him. He associated the man's blond hair with aristocracy.

Aw . . . he's really sweet. I think he's a sweetheart. I'm really, really, really starting to like this guy. There's something so . . . decent about him.

He stopped and reminded himself that the late pharaoh's high priest was also really, really dead.

CHAPTER EIGHT

"**B**es Ammon?" Jhonny kept repeating this over and over, as if it would all make sense and somehow sink in even though he was terrified that Chris would turn out to be a loon like Mike, he was fascinated. Best Man had told them some amazing things about ancient Egypt and history, and then . . . he'd vanished. Jhonny realized that this was the point he'd become afraid of the dead, of mysteries beyond the veil, petrified of *the other side.*

Ever sat in silence, looking miserable. Chris was the only one who thought the whole discovery was wonderful. He paced the room talking about how fantastic it all was that things were out in the open.

"Even my friend the cat is being acknowledged for his sacrifice in death. That's all he wanted, poor little guy. A bit of attention."

"What about you?" Jhonny asked. "What did you want?"

"Ever. I came back for Ever."

"God . . ." Ever stood.

"I've been waiting for so long," Chris said quickly." I was excited when the exhibit came here. I put the idea in Chris's head. I enjoyed hanging out with him. I popped in and out of his body. Imagine my surprise when he chased the two of you that day on the studio lot while I was inside him."

"I don't understand," Ever said. "I can't take it. I need air. I gotta get out of here. No offense, but I'm . . . I can't handle this."

"I'll walk with you," Chris offered.

"No!"

Chris adopted the wounded look again. An ancient Egyptian priest might have invaded Chris's body, but he was still . . . Chris.

"Let him go," Jhonny said. "Let him clear his head."

"Where is your mother?" Chris asked, as Ever walked toward the front door.

Ever turned, a sick look on his face. "I'm not talking about her with . . . *you*."

"Your father wants you to reconcile with her!" Chris shouted at Ever's retreating back. "He loves you!"

Jhonny glanced at his best friend, saw him pause, his back stiff, then watched him walk out the door without a backward glance.

"Why is he so upset?" Chris asked.

"Well, ya gotta admit it's all unusual," Jhonny said. He started to realize how weird it was that Ever loved dead people but had panicked and fled. Here was Jhonny talking to . . . Best Man!

"At least you're giving me a chance to explain," Chris said.

"Should I call you Chris or Bes Ammon?"

"Chris. For sure. Bes Ammon is dead . . . I'm Chris now." He blew out a sigh. "Things are worse than I thought between Ever and his mom."

"Yeah. They're pretty bad. I'd tread lightly there if I were you."

Chris frowned. "She still likes Ever's ex-boyfriend?"

Jhonny shook his head. "Likes him? She took Addison's side, even though he ripped Ever off, broke his heart and every other damned thing he could do to destroy him. She tells people Addison is the son she never had."

Chris was silent. "She's still his mother."

"There are bad mothers as well as good ones. She's a bad

one."

Chris shook his head. "No. She's a damaged mother. She made mistakes. Sometimes people don't know how to say they're sorry. I'd venture that Addison hurt her, too."

"She deserves it. Ever went through hell and she turned her back on him."

Chris said nothing for a moment. Then, "You're a loyal friend."

"I try to be."

Jhonny felt uncomfortable. He hated talking about Ever, or anyone he loved, behind their backs.

"I love him, too, you know, Jhonny."

"I'm gonna go talk to him." Jhonny turned off the computer.

"Can I come, too?"

"It's better you don't. Just give him a little time . . . okay?"

"Sure. And Jhonny? About Mike . . . there are plenty of other fish in the sea. He's all bark and no bite, but I'm glad you're okay. I won't let anything happen to you."

Jhonny stared at him for a moment. What he'd missed about their chats with Best Man was his humor and warmth. He'd felt hurt when Best Man vanished, and strange, sinister forces took his place. He realized now, he'd been feeling strangely abandoned by Best Man all these years.

"Guess I'll take a nap," Chris said, looking dejected. "Think I'll go into the bedroom. So much more comfortable in there."

Jhonny watched the man's sad gait. Now to find Ever. The car was still out front, but that didn't mean anything. In a city where nobody walked, he and Jhonny walked frequently. Even late at night. Where would he go at . . . he checked the time on his cell phone. Two-fifty in the morning?

He'd be in the guesthouse.

Jhonny pulled up his shirt collar in a vain effort to keep

out the frosty night air. LA was glorious by day, a frozen mess at night. He turned the corner of the building and felt the grass crunching in icy spikes under his shoes as he walked to the backyard. A dim light from the small windows showed him his first guess was correct. Ever was in there with all the stuff they kept in storage from boxes of books to their camera gear and collectibles.

He turned the door handle. It moved, the door finally giving way. Ever sat in a swivel chair by the lone desk in the cramped, single-room space and grinned.

"Care to join me?" He held up a bottle of Sambuca.

"Sure, I'd love it."

Jhonny smiled to himself. Ever had been drinking the licorice-flavored liqueur since their discovery of it in Greece the summer between high school graduation and the start of college.

He dropped three coffee beans into a shot glass, topping it with the clear liqueur. He lit a match and ignited the drink. The flame skittered across the top and evaporated.

They toasted each other.

"You okay?" Jhonny asked.

"Yeah. I went through the filing cabinet. I can't find the notes we took during our talks with Best Man."

"Didn't we toss them out?"

Ever shrugged. "I don't remember."

"Neither do I."

"It's some freaky shit, isn't it?"

"If we ever told anybody they'd think we were nuts."

Ever laughed. "They do anyway."

The liqueur tasted good. He took a couple of sips and glanced at the desktop.

"I think you're right about that. I see you have our notes out. You getting any work done on the new book?"

Ever grimaced. "Merely pretending, my friend."

"Too bad. I was looking forward to you finishing it all yourself. I was hoping just to see my name in print again and getting a couple of Amazon royalty checks down the line."

Ever laughed. "Jhonny. You're my best friend."

"Backatcha."

"Thanks for sticking by me."

"I'm with you, guy. Hit me with more Sambuca, will ya?"

Ever complied. "You really think he knows my father?"

"I dunno. So far everything he says seems . . . accurate. You should talk to him."

"I'm scared."

"What are you scared of most?"

"If he's an Egyptian invader . . . won't he have to leave again? I can't say goodbye again Jhonny. Too much heartbreak. It's left me . . . I dunno . . . "

"I know, buddy. Me, too. I loved your old man, too, you know. He was the best."

"Wasn't he?" Ever's face shone in the dark. "I miss him."

"Yeah, I know." Jhonny walked around the desk and sat on the arm of Johnny's swivel chair. They rarely talked about Ever's dad. His death had been horrible. Even Jhonny's parents took it hard. His mom even had a theory that Ever's mom had turned away from him not because she was really so crazy about Addison but because, Ever, the spitting image of his father was too painful a reminder of the man she had lost.

He'd never said so to Ever, but now, after all this time it sort of made sense.

"You suppose I should ask Chris about my dad?"

Ever's hopeful gaze tore at Jhonny.

"Yes," Jhonny said, taking his friend's hand and squeezing it. "I really, truly do."

"Chris?"

Ever sat on the edge of the bed. Chris turned around in the semi-darkness. The only light came from a street lamp outside. It cast an eerie glow around the room, but Ever didn't think he could handle full light. Not now.

Chris's body felt warm, strong and very reassuring.

"Hey, baby. I'm so glad you're back. Get in. You're freezing." He held open the bedcovers, but Ever was in turmoil.

"How is my dad?" he asked, fighting off tears. "It's only . . . I just . . . miss him so much and I know it sounds crazy because he's dead, but is he okay?"

Chris sat up and took his hands. Ever couldn't help it. The tears just roared up from his heart and fell out of his eyes.

"He's great. He's fantastic." Chris smiled at him. "He misses you." He glanced down at their joined hands. "He says he is very proud of the man you have become."

"Why did he have to die?" It was the one thing about life that sucked. The loneliness that came as a consequence of loss.

"Everyone dies, sweetheart." Chris's tone was gentle, and yes, his words were true.

"I wasn't ready to say goodbye."

"Nobody is, not even when it's . . . expected."

"He was my best friend."

Chris nodded. "I know."

Ever wiped the tears from his face. God, he was a mess. He needed tissues. He rose from the bed, but Chris held his hands.

"He said the passing was easy. You had a dog when you were a little boy, named Sammy."

Ever's mouth hung open. *Sammy.*

"Sammy was waiting for him."

"My God. I loved that dog. He loved to chase cars."

"Yes," Chris said. "I know."

"Sammy, his successor, Mitzi, Mitzi's successor Lindy and your cat, Tiana, were all waiting for him. Before he even saw his family, the animals were right there waiting for him."

Ever sobbed at the litany of names he'd loved and lost. Mitzi had died young, Lindy had been stolen from the backyard while he was at school one day, and his mom had accidentally run over Tiana one day. After that, Ever had put his foot down. No more animals. He couldn't handle fearing for their safety or losing them. But dear, sweet Sammy. Sammy had contracted heartworm after going back east with his dad. In those days, arsenic was the only cure. It had killed him. The sweet, little black dog with the white patch on his chest had just ballooned in weight one day, his body swelling with the nasty parasites squeezing his chest.

He had died at the vet's office in Ever's arms, his little body no longer tortured. Ever could still see his swollen belly, still feel the immediate stillness of the room when Sammy's soul left. That was why he and Jhonny had started fooling around with the Ouija board.

"Sammy's with him, and they'll be there waiting when it's your turn. They all love you on the other side."

Ever kept sobbing.

Chris squeezed Ever's hands harder, reaching forward and kissing his wet cheeks. "Don't do this. It's a celebration, sweetheart. He doesn't want you to be upset. He's waited a long time to let you know he loves you and they're all waiting. They watch over you."

Ever couldn't stand it. His heart was breaking into a million pieces. The pain of being able to talk about his father again was like lancing a wound. It hurt, but my God, years of pain tumbled from his very soul. His mother never wanted to talk about him. She threw away anything that had belonged to him, got rid of it all. Ever had been able to salvage only one suit jacket and his father's golf cap. He had also discovered one photo she had missed when she set fire to his papers. They'd fought over it. He thought at the time her denial and grief were so deep that she went on her rampage of destruction because of it.

Chris paused and seemed to be listening. "He's worried about your mom. She's not well but doesn't know it. He wants you to help her."

Ever thought about his mother and the corrupted nature of their relationship. They rarely spoke. Would she even listen to him?

Chris nodded again, his head down, muttering something under his breath. He glanced up at Ever.

"Please, he says. Do this for him."

"He asks too much."

"No." Chris shook his head. "The right time will come. We'll find a way. In the meantime, can I hold you now, please?"

Ever pulled himself away, got some tissues from the bathroom and took a moment for himself. Back in the bedroom, he slipped off his shoes and got between the sheets, allowing Chris to comfort him. All he could think in his frozen, hysterical state was how wrong God got it over and over again, allowing beautiful, innocent animals and sweet little children to suffer cruelly while some humans like serial killers and pedophiles lived illness-free lives. Why?

He let Chris infuse warmth into his frozen body and smiled as Chris covered his face with kisses. Just as he thought he'd never feel warm again, he did. And then something curved into his tailbone. He gasped, holding his breath. He heard the distinct sound of purring.

Tiana.

Jhonny opened up Crazy Pie's kitchen to the early-morning deliveries. He had no idea why, but he felt compelled to do this. He felt strangely good, the kind of good that usually came from a hot night of sex and little sleep. He'd had little sleep but had spent the few hours he caught some z's dreaming about some nameless, faceless guy who kissed him, telling him to wait.

He longed to tell Ever . . . then realized Ever was still in bed. He wondered how his best friend was doing with Chris and was surprised when a small black dog showed up. The poor thing looked starving, with the puffy belly but otherwise skinny, raggedy form that came with severe malnutrition. The dog was a little skittish, but Jhonny coaxed him into the kitchen, feeding him torn strips of chicken. He licked Johnny's hand.

Jhonny fell in love. He knew that Ever had a no-pet rule, but Jhonny wanted the little black dog. He called Ever, who answered the phone sleepily.

"A black dog, you say?"

Jhonny held his breath, excited at the excitement in Ever's voice.

"Keep him there. I'm on my way."

Jhonny worried about somebody finding the dog in the kitchen and reporting him to the Food and Drug Authority. Or worse. His mom. However, the dog found himself a spot between food sacks in the walk-in pantry and lay, head on his paws, watching Jhonny walk.

When Ever arrived fifteen minutes later, the dog wagged his tail when Ever picked him up, laughing as the puppy licked his face.

"What should we call him?" Jhonny asked.

"Ammon?" Ever asked. "I think somehow this little guy was the result of some divine intervention.

"Sounds good to me," Jhonny said. He watched the way

Ever interacted with the puppy, who strained to get his tongue on Jhonny's face, too.

"What a character."

Ever nodded. "I had a dog just like him once."

"Yeah! Sammy! That's funny. Except Sammy had a white splash on his chest."

Ever turned Ammon over in his arms. "He has it on his belly."

"He's starving," Ever said.

"This little guy won't be starving for long. Where's Chris?"

"In the car waiting. We'll go to PETCO and load up on stuff for him."

The dog seemed to understand, and Jhonny was certain he smiled at him over Ever's shoulder.

Jhonny turned to find his mother standing beside him, hands on hips.

"Please don't tell me I just saw a dog in my kitchen."

"All right, if you like. You didn't see a dog in the kitchen."

Rosa laughed and pinched his cheeks.

"I've seen that dog around for a few days, but he'd never come near me," she said.

"You don't have the magic touch, I guess."

She punched his arm playfully. "What are you doing here so early?"

"I dunno. Thought I'd come and help."

"Did you now?" His mom grinned as the delivery truck rolled up to the back door. "We'll unload everything, and I'll cook us a nice breakfast, okay?"

"Okay." It was better than okay. For some reason, he was excited to be here. He wanted to help. He worked with his mom and was pleased when Vanessa arrived to a job completed.

"Why don't you go spend a bit more time with Darren and Ivy?" he asked.

"Oh, no. The mornings are their special times together. I don't want to take that away from her."

Her face crumpled a little. "She's adorable though, isn't she?"

"Gorgeous," Jhonny said. He thought it was nice that his sister was willing to give Ivy some private time with her dad.

"The three of us are having a picnic tomorrow up at Lake Castaic. I've never been there." She looked worried. "Mom . . . I should have checked with you first. Will you be okay? I mean—"

"I'll help out," Jhonny insisted.

"You will?" Vanessa looked stunned.

"What about your new museum project?" his mom asked.

"I can do both. Besides, I want to be here."

"Just for that, I'll even make your favorite flapjacks," Vanessa said, tying on an apron.

"Oh, boy." Jhonny couldn't remember the last time Vanessa had made him flapjacks.

"I'll put the coffee on," Rose said.

All three of them hummed different tunes that, strangely, didn't seem out of place together. It was kind of like how things were with him, his mom and his sister. Three-voice harmony of a different kind.

Ever had forgotten the unique and wonderful smell of puppy breath. The dog in his arms seemed to know he'd been saved. He clung to the little guy, images of Sammy coming back to him. Sammy had been a stray, too. He'd asked Chris three times if Ammon was Sammy coming back to him, each time Chris gave him some enigmatic response.

Not that it mattered. He'd missed having a dog.

"Mrs. Zapel," he said, suddenly. "She'll go mad. We're not supposed to have animals there."

"I'll talk to her. I'll persuade her."

Ever didn't argue. He trusted and believed Chris. They pulled up at PETCO, the puppy anxious to pee. Ever found a patch of grass outside the building. The puppy squatted, then raced right back to Ever, his ears flapping, just like Sammy. He tried not to think about Sammy and just laughed as the puppy tongue bathed his face again. He thought about all the things he had to do. Take the dog to the vet and get him checked and vaccinated.

He had to feed him. He and Chris loaded up a cart with a dog bed, food, toys, bowls, a collar, and leash. They made a tag for him, and when they paid for all their items, Chris insisted on paying. They even got a PETCO club card in both their names.

The dog licked their hands as they knelt and put the new collar on him.

"I have a meeting with the investors of the museum tonight," Ever said, getting to his feet. He'd avoided all conversation on the topic with Chris because he hadn't been sure about involving him. Chris stood after putting the leash on Ammon's collar. They took the dog's new stash to the car trunk, stowed it, and he reached for Chris's hand.

"Let's walk."

They did, trudging in companionable silence for a moment.

"I'm still adjusting to everything," Ever said, searching for the right way to broach the subject.

"Yes, sweetheart, I know."

"And I'm still not sure I get everything. But . . . I'm willing to see how things . . . go."

"Thank you." Chris seemed pleased. "I know it's . . . unusual, but I want to make you happy, Ever. Please believe me."

"I do. I actually think you do. We talked about you investing in the museum—"

"And I still want to, but just so you know, I'm going to apply for the police academy again. This time I'll get in."

Ever stared at him. "You really want to do that?"

Chris smiled, pausing to let Ammon sniff another dog's squirt site on a streetlamp.

"Well," he said, "Chris does. It's been his dream. He . . . well, how do I put this?"

"Just say it?"

"He wasn't really bright enough to pass the written exam, and his personality wasn't exactly desirable. I, however, am brilliant."

Ever grinned. "If you do say so yourself."

"I don't believe in false modesty, Ever. I was the personal physician of a ruling pharaoh, and I also taught his sons. I was the priest for his religion, and I made his love spells so he could win his concubines."

"So you are a love god!"

"Yeah." Chris grinned. "The point is, I come from an ancient culture, a civilization that created monuments the likes of which have never been seen before or since my time. I've waited a long time to come back and help." His eyes glittered for a moment, the emotion evident. "I was granted this wish because I was murdered. And they have let me stay here because I have proven that I mean no harm, I mean only good."

"Kind of like an angel getting his wings?"

"Oh." Chris rolled his eyes. "So flippant. Sort of like that, but the way I see it is this. Chris was kind enough to let me take over his body, so I feel I owe him. I also think with my powers, I'd made a damned fine cop."

Ever stared at him, in awe. "I think you would, too."

"And I can still invest in your business. Chris saved a lot of money." He grinned. "I mean, *I* saved a lot of money."

Ever nodded. "So we each do our own thing and we still . . ."

"We still get to spend our free time together. You think you'd like that?"

They watched their new puppy hunch over to poop.

"Yeah," Ever said. "I think I'd like that. A lot."

Jhonny and Ever called the meeting to order. Mrs. Zapel had fallen all over the new puppy — and Ivy Moon — and was baby and puppy sitting for the duration. The little guy thought all their collectibles were his personal chew toys and Ivy Moon wanted to be wherever Ammon was.

The two roommates couldn't discuss business and keep an eye on the puppy at the same time. Darren couldn't discuss business, keep his eye on Vanessa and eat all at the same time, and Mrs. Zapel offered to help. With things more or less quiet, Ever addressed the group of thirty people squeezed into their living room. After the meeting was over, they'd put everything away again before Ammon could sink his teeth into them.

They planned to show everyone a virtual tour of the new facility. Amazing what you could do with a computer and a projector.

Ever frowned for a moment. Chris was glaring at him. Probably still sulking over their brief argument in the kitchen when he'd asked Chris why he couldn't do something to stop the puppy from chewing.

"Because I can't," had been his response. "My thing is engines. I could always teach the little guy how to fly!"

"No. No flying! I thought you said you were a genius."

"I never said that. I said I was brilliant, and brilliant is not perfect," Chris had said.

And now Chris still seemed really mad at him.

Their living room was filled with people who oohed and aahed over their treasure trove of finds. Vanessa had outdone herself with finger foods. She passed around bite-size pizza rounds, dimpling with pleasure at the compliments she received.

"She's my girlfriend," Darren kept telling people.

Vanessa ran next door with extra food for Ivy and Mrs. Zapel. "Don't start without me," she called over her shoulder.

And so they waited.

When Vanessa rushed back, she squeezed beside Darren. Jhonny passed out their proposal in binders to everyone present.

On a white screen against the wall, they ran the virtual tour that Ever and Jhonny knew was spectacular. They had digitally inserted images of their best pieces into the cavernous space. They'd also provided a PowerPoint presentation, which Ever could tell impressed everyone, and then came the questions.

"How are you going to work out security for all the museum items?" somebody asked. "Ever since that mummy went missing at the science museum it's worried me."

"Our new head of security is Chris Coelho," Ever surprised himself by announcing to everybody.

He noticed out of the corner of his eye that Chris sat up a little straighter. "Yes," he said. "The cost is factored into the presentation, but I have plans that will be state-of-the-art, and," he said, with a dramatic pause, "will be both unconventional and . . . brilliant."

Ever grinned at him. "I'm sure they will."

"Guaranteed." Chris winked at him. "And I will build a

golden motorcycle that flies around the museum. No other museum has anything like it."

"I don't doubt that," Ever said. He and Jhonny fielded a lot more questions, and after the meeting was over, they spent more time with those who chose to stay and wanted more details. They were stunned that every single one of the attendees wanted to invest.

"It's awesome," Chris said. "You did great, guys."

"We did?" Ever was still worried. He and Jhonny could rent the space and begin the renovation process, but he still worried about how Addison would handle the news of Ever returning to the tour business. He was bound to find out sooner or later.

"You leave that asshole to me," Chris said.

"Really?"

"Yes, really." Chris leaned in and kissed him. Things turned hot very fast.

"Guys," Jhonny whined. "Can you turn off the oven for a moment? It's hot in here, and we need to put stuff away before Ammon comes back."

Too late. The puppy romped in, his ears flapping madly and his little mouth clamped down the leg of the *I Love Lucy* sofa.

"Oh, no you don't." Chris swooped the pup into his arms. They seemed to have some silent conversation. "I thought so," Chris said. He put the dog back down.

"What did he say?" Ever asked before he could stop himself. *What am I saying? He's a dog . . . but still . . . I think they communicate.*

"He said he wants an extra walk tonight and he will be a good boy and not chew if he can sleep with us."

"Did he really say all that?"

"Of course."

"And he'll stop chewing?"

"I told him we'd get him some bones tomorrow."

"Huh. You're quite the negotiator, aren't you?"

"Oh, boy." Jhonny snorted. "You two are just a little too gooey if you don't mind my saying. Anyway, I thought Ammon was my dog?"

"He's our dog. We all love him," Ever said.

Jhonny grinned. "So I still have a home here in spite of how hot and heavy you guys are now?"

"What are you kidding? You're my best friend, idiot." Ever reached over and hugged him.

Jhonny responded, then gave him a slight push.

"Go get your groove on, and I'll finish up in here."

Ever grinned at him. "Thanks, Jhonny."

"*No es nada.*"

"We gotta get him a guy," Chris whispered as they ran off to their room, the pup at their heels.

Jhonny called for Ammon, who turned and ran off again. They closed the door. Later, much later when it was time to sleep, Ever would share the bed with Chris, little Ammon wedged between them. For now, however, making love with Chris had become Ever's obsession.

"Do we have to use rubbers?" Chris asked.

"Until we get tested, yes. But I can't wait to have you inside me."

"And I can't wait to be inside you. I love making you come hard, Ever."

He took Ever into his arms. Nothing else mattered. He couldn't wait to get Chris naked.

"I'm really in love with this body," Ever said.

Damn. I said it. The l word.

He raised his eyes from Chris's pecs to the man's eyes. Their gazes held.

"Is that all you love?" Chris asked.

"No."

Chris grinned, taking Ever's face into his hands. His kiss was soulful and deep.

"I want to love you and take care of you, Ever. Do you remember any of the things I said to you in the Ouija board session?"

Ever shook his head.

"I said I would come back. I told you I had to leave. I crossed boundaries in the spirit world. They made me stay away. I said I would find a way to come back. I said, *For Ever*. I meant for you. I also meant *forever*. I wanna be here for you."

Ever put his hand on Chris's bare, naked torso and loved the feel of the man's skin.

"I know it's only been a short time that we've been together," Chris said, "but it hasn't. Not really. We knew each other a long, long time ago and we got separated."

"My God . . . are you . . . serious?"

"I'm not telling you any of this to scare you. I'm saying, things will come back to you, and I'll be right here. But none of that matters. Cosmic history . . . destiny . . ." He paused. "Determination . . . none of it really means a tin of beans. What matters is how it feels when I'm with you and when I am . . . wow, Ever. Nobody has made me feel the way you do. I love you."

He kissed Ever with such passion that Ever thought he would come just from mouth-to-mouth contact. They fell on the bed naked, their puppy scratching outside the door.

"Walkies," Jhonny called out, and Ammon raced off in a flurry of barks.

"Mmmm . . . now . . . where we?" Chris put Ever onto his back, licking his jutting cock, which leaked over both their bellies. He worked his way down the shaft, Ever crying out as Chris sucked in one of his balls, then the other. Chris and his magic tongue.

"What's a *ka*?" Ever suddenly asked. He'd kept meaning to ask, but things had happened so fast, and with the investors' meeting . . . he kept remembering stuff he wanted to know.

"A *ka*?" Chris came off his ass long enough to give him a rueful smile. "You need to know this right now?"

Ever shrugged, stroking his lover's head.

Chris tilted his face and kissed Ever's hand. "It's a part of the soul. Like a double. We believed, in ancient Egypt, that your soul is put into an object when you pass."

"And you lost your soul?" Ever was trying to understand.

Chris grinned, kissing along Ever's thigh. "I was very uncoordinated at first if you recall. I had no idea where I was, and Chris sometimes resisted me. Until you accepted him, that is. So yes, I found my *ka*. I have you."

Chris dropped his head again, licking him at a leisurely pace. Ever was surprised when Chris released his cock and moved between his thighs.

"Open them for me," he said. "Now."

Ever couldn't have resisted him if he'd tried. Chris sent him to heights that no one ever had.

"Don't leave me," he said.

"I won't. I promise."

He saw the tears on Chris's face.

"You know who I am and you still want me," Chris said.

"Yes, I do."

Chris licked and sucked at Ever's asshole.

"I can't wait," he moaned. "I wanna take my time, but I need you, Ever."

"Take me. Fuck me. I want you."

Chris slipped on a rubber and sliced into him. Ever's body arched up to Chris's relentless thrusts. A few seconds of pain cascaded into splendor. Ever saw a golden place. It took his breath away. He saw magic and fire and a face he knew was the real Bes Ammon.

"Oh, fuck . . . Chris, you were . . . are . . . lovely."

"Show me. Show me you want me."

Ever held onto him, opening himself up to Chris. His cock rubbed against his lover's hard, flat belly.

"Oh . . . you're beautiful," Chris said in his ear, again and again, moving against Ever in a hula-hip fashion, which only inflamed the surge of desire Ever experienced. He grabbed Chris's hips.

"Fuck, I'm coming, I'm coming!"

Chris's mouth clamped down on his, the ancient love god of forever in his mind, bowing. Ever heard the man saying, *I am at your service. Always. Here. I am here for you. For Ever.*

The love god of forever. Or, as Ever liked to think of him, the love god of Indian frybread.

Ever would have the rest of his life, he hoped, to discover what it would all mean. And to show the love god how much he could love him back.

ABOUT THE AUTHOR

A.J. Llewellyn divides her time between California and Hawaii. Bags of Kona coffee in the fridge and a healthy collection of Hawaiian records keep her refueled when she is on the mainland.

A. J.'s passion for the islands led her to writing a play about the last ruling monarch of Hawaii, Queen Lili'uokalani. She has also written a non-erotic novel about the overthrow of her kingdom—in diary form from her maid's point of view.

She never lacks inspiration for male/male erotic romances and has to force her fingers from the computer keyboard to pursue other passions: collecting books on Hawaiiana, surfing and spending time with family, friends and her animal companions.

A.J. Llewellyn believes that love is a song best sung out loud. To find out more about A. J., visit her website at http://www.ajllewellyn.com, or you can reach her at aj@ajllewellyn.com.